TOMORROW'S BLOSSOMS

When Shelagh Muir's Doctor husband is sent to prison she starts afresh with her family in a new town, helped by James, the man who loved her before she married Gregory. She is happy and content — until the day Gregory comes home. Will Shelagh win her struggle to keep the security she had built up, and which of the two men in her life will she choose?

BEATRICE TAYLOR

TOMORROW'S BLOSSOMS

Complete and Unabridged

LINFORD
Leicester

First published in Great Britain in 1971 by
Robert Hale Limited
London

First Linford Edition
published September 1992

British Library CIP Data

Taylor, Beatrice
Tomorrow's blossoms.—Large print ed.—
Linford romance library
I. Title II. Series
823.914 [F]

ISBN 0–7089–7277–2

Published by
F. A. Thorpe (Publishing) Ltd.
Anstey, Leicestershire

Set by Words & Graphics Ltd.
Anstey, Leicestershire
Printed and bound in Great Britain by
T. J. Press (Padstow) Ltd., Padstow, Cornwall

1

"THERE, dear." Shelagh Muir fitted the satin coronet with its orange blossom trimming carefully onto the bouffant veil through which her daughter's bright hair gleamed like pale gold.

Then she carefully straightened the slim, almost severe lines of the wedding dress, before standing back, her eyes full of love and pride.

"You look really beautiful, Di."

Diane regarded herself critically in the long mirror.

"Mm. Not bad at all. Dorothy's surpassed herself this time. My dress is absolutely fab, and having your wedding veil just finishes it off. How clever of you to keep it all this time."

"Twenty-two years."

Shelagh blinked, feeling the tears gather in her eyes as she looked back

1

down that long tunnel of time, seeing as if through the wrong end of a telescope the young and eager girl she had been then.

She had been so happy, so much in love, a love which she had been sure would last for ever. Had ever a bride, before or since, been so naïve, so immature, she asked herself wryly.

"Now, Mom, remember your promise." Diane's anxious voice roused her, bringing her back with a jerk to the present. "No tears on my wedding day. Don't spoil it with regrets."

"Of course I won't, Di. It's just seeing you in my veil, looking so lovely and so young — "

"Young? I'm twenty-one. Three years older than you were when you got married, don't forget."

"That's true. You were nearly two years old before I had my twenty-first birthday, and here you are, getting married yourself. It doesn't seem possible."

"She looks just like you do in your

2

wedding photo, Mummy."

Shelagh smiled at her younger daughter, who was already wearing her golden yellow bridesmaid's dress and looked quite unlike her usual untidy self.

"I do believe you're right, Kate. Whatever happened to that old photo? I haven't seen it since we moved here."

"I've got it."

"You?" Diane looked at her in astonishment. "What on earth do you want it for? You do the queerest things sometimes, Kate. Go and get it and let's have a look at it."

"No. There isn't time now," Shelagh said quickly.

The last thing she wanted on that day when she was holding on only precariously to her composure, was to see that picture of herself and Gregory. That reminder of what she had thought was the beginning of an idyllic happiness but which, in the end, had brought her only heartbreak and frustration.

3

"Of course there is." Diane's mouth set in the obstinate lines her mother knew so well. "I want to see it."

"But James will be here soon."

Her daughter looked at her sharply, then bent and kissed her.

"Sorry, Mom. I forgot for the moment. You certainly wouldn't want that old photo lying around when he comes, especially as he's going to give me away."

"Daddy ought to be doing that," Kate said loudly.

Her sister sighed in exasperation.

"Honestly, you must be crazy. How on earth could he?"

"They might have let him come, if Mom had asked them."

"Might they? Very nice, too. I can just see the write-up in the local paper. 'The bride's father was allowed out of gaol to give his daughter away.' No, thank you very much."

"I'd sooner have him than James, any day."

"That's enough, Kate."

Shelagh spoke sharply, aware that both her daughters were thinking the same thing though with widely differing reactions, and that nothing she could say would convince them that they were wrong. That however fond she was of James, she was not yet convinced that she loved him enough to marry him, as she knew he wanted her to.

"James has been a very good friend to us all," she went on, quietly. "I hope you won't say anything to upset him. He's been so looking forward to today."

Kate hunched her shoulders.

"I won't. I won't talk to him at all."

Her mother sighed.

"That's almost as bad. Don't spoil Di's day for her, love."

"She couldn't," Diane said confidently. "Nobody could."

"Don't be too sure, Di." Shelagh felt a stab of fear, a superstitious desire to cross her fingers. "Don't tempt Providence."

"Oh, Mom, you're the end! There's

no need to worry about Neil and me. We're going to be madly happy."

Shelagh was aware of a dull ache of longing, almost of jealousy, within her. If only she had had that arrogant self-confidence. That certainty that nothing could go wrong for her. Perhaps things might have been different.

But she had not. And even now, at nearly forty, she still did not have it, as she told James ruefully when he arrived a few minutes later.

He smiled down at her.

"I'm very pleased to hear it. I wouldn't want you to be any different, Shelagh."

"Thank you, James. You always say the right thing. I can't tell you how grateful I am to you for everything you've done for us."

"Whatever I have done has been for you," he said with emphasis.

She coloured, her mind as always shying away from the implication behind his words, unwilling to face the truth which was that James's help

6

had not been completely disinterested.

She knew he was still remembering the time when their families had hoped they would marry, before she had met Gregory. After that there had been no place in her life for James. Except as a friend.

He put his hands on each side of her head, turning her face towards him, his eyes concerned.

"Is anything the matter, Shelagh? What's worrying you? Is it Brian?"

"No, of course not. He seems to have settled down at last. He even put on the morning suit I hired for him without too much grumbling, and went off like a lamb to the church to do his 'ushering'."

"But there's something wrong," he insisted. "What is it, my dear?"

"Nothing, really. Just that I've suddenly realised how much I'm going to miss Di. She's been a wonderful help to me since — since Gregory went away."

He frowned, his lips tightening in annoyance.

"So that's it! You're thinking about him. When are you going to learn, Shelagh?"

"No, I'm not. I was just remembering my own wedding day and thinking how very young I was then. Not nearly ready for marriage. No wonder it went wrong."

"You're not to blame for that."

"I am, partly, anyway," she said honestly. "I didn't even begin to understand how important Gregory's work was to him. That when it came to a choice between it and me, I came a very poor second. And how I resented it!"

He moved impatiently.

"Nonsense. It was entirely his fault. He neglected you and the children. He never wanted to go out with you. You know that's true."

"A doctor isn't as free as other men, James."

"That wasn't the reason. Do you think he's going to be any different now he isn't a doctor any longer?

Now he's been struck off? Convicted of leaving a child to die?"

"That isn't true! Mom, why do you let him say such things?"

Shelagh whirled round to see her younger daughter standing still in the doorway, her round, still childish face flushed with anger.

"Kate, remember what you promised," she said sharply. "What do you want?"

Kate's mouth set mutinously and for a moment Shelagh thought she was on the brink of another clash between her daughter and James. Then she breathed a sigh of relief when Kate only said,

"The car's here and I can't find my flowers."

"They're in the kitchen. Come along and I'll get them for you." She turned apologetically to James. "Go up to Diane, will you? She's waiting for you."

When she came back from seeing Kate leave for the church she was glad to find the sitting room empty.

She needed a little time to herself to overcome the depression which was

9

threatening to spoil all her pleasure in Diane's wedding day. A depression which had taken her by surprise and which seemed to be deepening every minute.

She had been so sure she had put the past firmly behind her. Yet it had needed only the smallest reminder to bring memories crowding back, even those she had thought were buried for ever deep below the surface of her mind.

She closed her eyes, thinking how impossible it would have seemed then, on her wedding day, that she would ever cease to love Gregory.

Yet she had; and though she had made a new life for herself and the children far away from the place where Gregory's practice had been, she knew she had lost something precious. That she would never again recapture the joy and happiness of those early years, before they had lost touch with each other.

She heard the door open and turned,

expecting to see Diane and James. So that the shock was even greater than it would have been, as she stared at the man smiling uncertainly at her from just inside the room, the streak of silver standing out starkly against the darkness of his hair.

"Aren't you going to say hello?" he said at last, breaking the silence that was becoming almost tangible between them.

Shelagh let out her breath sharply, feeling the blood tingle painfully through her, still scarcely believing her eyes.

"Gregory! You!"

He came further into the room, hesitantly as though unsure of his welcome, and put down the raincoat and case he was carrying.

"Yes, it's me. Home again, Shelagh. For good this time, I hope."

Her eyes widened in dismay.

"But you can't come home. Not today."

He frowned, the lines beside his mouth deepening.

"Why not?" he asked harshly.

"Because it's too soon. There's another six months to go before — "

His face lighted up with relief.

"Good conduct," he finished wryly.

"Released?" She pressed her hands over her eyes, trying to quiet the pounding in her head which was making it difficult for her to think. "I'm sorry, Gregory. You must think I'm crazy. If only you'd let me know you were coming."

"I thought I'd surprise you. I suppose that wasn't a very bright idea."

"No, not really. You should have written."

He glanced at her.

"We were neither of us very good at that, were we?"

She coloured, recognising the accusation behind his words, and said defensively,

"That wasn't my fault. I wrote regularly at first but you didn't reply. You wouldn't even see me when I came to visit you."

"I'm not blaming you, Shelagh, or myself," he said wearily. "You see I was ill for a time — "

"Ill? What was the matter with you? Why wasn't I told?"

"I wouldn't let them tell you."

"Why not?" She moved restlessly, trying to suppress the irritation and resentment she felt at his words. "I don't understand you, Gregory."

He shrugged.

"That's nothing new, is it? Maybe I thought you wouldn't be interested or perhaps I just wasn't thinking straight. You see, they found I had a depressed fracture of the skull."

"A fractured skull? But how?"

"Probably by cracking my head against the windscreen or the car roof when the accident happened." He touched the silver streak across his hair. "That's what caused this."

She looked at him in dawning comprehension.

"Then all the time — at the trial — is that why you were so strange?"

"I suppose so."

She frowned, trying without very much success to adjust to this new knowledge, feeling as if the conversation was taking place in a dream. That it was not really happening at all.

"But you're all right now?" she asked, and then was appalled at the triteness of her question.

He hesitated, then said boldly, "Yes."

She was aware of a feeling of reserve behind that short answer, as if he was hiding something from her, then dismissed the suspicion impatiently.

She was imagining things, that was all, because of the sudden shock of hearing about his injury. He would not now hide the truth from her as he would have done in the early years of their marriage, when he had always tried to shelter her from pain and unhappiness.

"That's good," she said at last, "though I still don't understand why you didn't tell me afterwards, when you were better."

"I meant to, as soon as I saw you, but you didn't come."

She felt a surge of anger at his words, an anger which effectively dispersed the constraint which, up to that moment, had been making her feel as if she was talking to a complete stranger instead of her own husband.

"I couldn't help that! I had so much to do, selling the practice and the house, coming to live here. It was such a long journey, too."

He moved impatiently.

"Whose fault was that? There was no need to move so far away. Surely you could have found somewhere suitable nearer to Greetham?"

"We couldn't stay there, where everybody knew — what had happened," she flashed. "And the shop was here."

"Oh, yes, the shop." He sounded amused. "I can't imagine you as a business woman, Shelagh."

She flushed, annoyed by his attitude.

"I had to learn. It wasn't easy but I

did it, and I've made a success of it, too," she said proudly.

His expression softened.

"Sorry, love. I know how hard you must have worked, but now I'm home I'll be able to take some of the responsibilities off your shoulders."

Her eyes darkened in dismay.

"But you can't stay here."

"Why can't I?" he asked sharply.

"Because — " She swallowed nervously. "Because everyone thinks you deserted us."

She was surprised by his sudden crack of laughter.

"You have got yourself into a pickle, haven't you? What on earth made you tell people that?"

"I didn't tell them. They thought it and I didn't deny It. You must see I couldn't let them know the truth. It wouldn't have been fair to the children."

"The children! That's all you ever think about, isn't it? Well, they're not children any longer. It's time they

16

learned that life isn't all beer and skittles. You can't shelter them for ever, Shelagh."

"I haven't tried to. They had to face up to what happened while we were living in Greetham. There was no reason why they should still have to here, where nobody knew us."

He moved restlessly.

"I suppose you're right."

"I know I am" she said quietly. "You can see, then, why you can't stay here."

He turned to face her, his mouth stern.

"No, I can't. There's no real problem, Shelagh. You can tell them I've come back." He smiled suddenly, and she saw a glint in his eyes which reminded her of the husband she had known in the first happy years of their marriage. "The prodigal husband has returned to the fold."

"How can I? It wouldn't be true."

"Why not?" His voice took on a more urgent note. "Can't we forget the past, love? Start again here, in this new place?"

She shook her head.

"No. It's too late for that."

He moved to her, taking her hands firmly in his.

"It isn't, Shelagh. We were happy together once. We can be again."

"That was a long time ago, Gregory. You can't turn back the clock. I've made a new life for myself now."

She looked straight at him as she spoke and saw with sadness the lost look in his eyes, wishing she need not hurt him even while she knew there was nothing else she could do.

Then the look was gone, replaced by a flash of intense anger, as he said deliberately,

"And there's no room in it for me?"

"I didn't say that!"

"No, but it's what you meant, isn't it?" he asked harshly. Then his mood changed and he said eagerly, "But I won't believe it. You can't have

18

changed so much. Shelagh!"

He moved suddenly and caught hold of her, pulling her close against him. His mouth came down on hers, hard and demanding, seeking a response that she knew she could not give him. That she did not dare to give if she was to retain the peace of mind which she had gained so painfully over the past months.

She stiffened in his arms, trying to break away from him, and when at last he released her, she staggered and would have fallen if he had not steadied her.

She stood for a moment, fighting the anger which surged inside her. Then as he moved away and she recognised the defeated droop to his shoulders, she felt the resentment begin to die away and was aware of a momentary urge to go to him and try to comfort him.

But that impulse was gone in a moment, because she knew she must not deceive him about her real feelings. It was kinder to let him know at once that their life together was over; that there was no longer any need for either of them to go through the unhappiness of the past years again, those years when they had gradually drifted farther and farther away from each other.

The time had come for her to be strong and truthful, to put an end to things completely, for his sake as well as her own.

He turned and looked at her, his eyes stern and bleak, then said at last, breaking the silence between them,

"So, I was wrong?"

"Yes," she began, then as he took a step towards her, she backed away, feeling an irrational stab of fear.

He stopped at once, his mouth twisting sardonically.

"There's no need to be afraid, Shelagh. I won't try to kiss you again. At least, not until you ask me to. And don't you think you'd better straighten your hat? It would never do for anyone to suspect that your husband has been making love to you."

The colour flamed into her face at the contempt in his voice and she put up unsteady hands to do as he said.

He watched her frowningly, then a look of awareness came into his eyes, as if realisation had only just come to him.

"Why are you all dressed up anyway? Going somewhere special?"

"To Di's wedding," she said baldly, then when she saw the expression on his face she was sorry she had not broken that news to him more gently.

But the look of pain was gone almost as soon as it appeared and his voice was steady as he said sharply,

"And nobody bothered to tell me about it? Well now, isn't that lucky? I've got here just in time to give her away."

Shelagh felt panic surge through her at his words and put out her hand to him.

"No, you can't. Di doesn't want you to!"

His mouth tightened.

"She'd rather forget she's got a father. Is that it?"

"You can't blame her if she feels like that," she said defensively. "Or Brian, either. They were both old enough to be hurt by what people said, the way they acted."

He did not reply for a moment, only looked at her in a way which made it difficult for her to meet his eyes.

Then he shrugged and said coldly,

"I don't blame them, Shelagh. You're the one I blame. You didn't believe in my innocence, you condemned me even before you heard the evidence, so it's hardly surprising if everybody else did, too."

"That isn't true!" she cried, trying to find the words in which to explain to him why she had found it so difficult to give him the trust and love which she had been losing so gradually over the years before that awful day when the police had come to the house.

But they did not come. She did not

22

know how to tell him that he himself had made it impossible for her to think him anything else but guilty. That his behaviour both before and during his trial had convinced her of his guilt.

Yet even as she hesitated she felt a deep compassion for him, standing there in his old suit, looking lonely and somehow defenceless, and with a sudden desire to give him some crumb of comfort she said quickly,

"Everybody didn't condemn you, Gregory. Kate didn't."

She saw the sudden light in his eyes and was glad that she had said those words.

"Didn't she? I hoped — when she wrote to me — but I couldn't really be sure. My little Kate. Is she here, Shelagh?"

"No, she's away to the church. She's Di's bridesmaid," she said, and saw the light die away as he remembered.

He walked over to the window and stood looking out, one hand thrust into his pocket in the characteristic way she knew so well.

At last he turned towards her and said quietly,

"Who's giving Di away? You?"

She shook her head.

"No. James."

The lines beside his mouth deepened.

"Seaton? Your strait-laced cousin?"

"He isn't my cousin," she said sharply.

"Well, second cousin twice removed. What does it matter? And why him?"

"Because he wanted it. He's been very good to me — to us. He found me this house and the shop. I don't know how we'd have managed but for him."

"He seems to have taken over all my responsibilities," he said sardonically. "But that's something he always wanted to do, isn't it, Shelagh?"

"You know that isn't true!" she said sharply, and felt a surge of relief as the doorbell pealed at that moment, knowing she could not have stood the

24

strain of this difficult meeting for very much longer without breaking down. "That will be the car for me. I'll have to go, Gregory."

"I think I'll come with you."

"No, you mustn't!"

He shrugged.

"Don't worry, I'm not serious. I wouldn't want to spoil things for you and Di. Not today, at least."

She looked up at him questioningly, trying to interpret his meaning, but without success.

"It's only for her sake, Gregory. It would be too unexpected, too upsetting for her — "

"There's no need to explain. I understand perfectly," he said wearily, and walked over to the door and opened it for her.

"Thank you." She hesitated in the doorway. "Gregory, I'm sorry. I wish it didn't have to be like this — "

"Leave it, Shelagh," he interrupted sharply.

She stood for a moment, then as

the bell rang out again went past him quickly, hardly knowing what she was doing.

Over the past months she had never faced up to what would happen when Gregory came out of prison, so that now she was completely unprepared and deeply afraid.

How would Diane and Brian react to their father's unexpected appearance, she thought miserably, as the car conveyed her quickly towards the church. What effect would it have on them, especially on Brian who was only just getting over the difficult phase which had followed his enforced change of school and the shock of realising that the father he had hero-worshipped was not the demi-god he had thought him, but as human and vulnerable as everybody else?

And the friends she had made since coming to Beilton. Were they now going to find out the truth? The truth which she had kept from them all so carefully.

2

GREGORY watched from the window as Shelagh got into the car, then when it finally disappeared from view, turned back into the room, feeling weary and disillusioned.

He had come home full of hope, but now that hope had disappeared. evaporating without trace in the first few minutes of his meeting with his wife.

He moved restlessly, admitting honestly to himself that he had been mad to expect to take up his life with Shelagh where it had been left off. He ought to have known that it was just not feasible, especially as the slow weeks passed and she did not visit him. Only he had not.

Instead he had told himself that it was his own fault because he had refused to

see her when he was in hospital. He had convinced himself without difficulty that it was the distance she had to travel and the fact that now she was the only breadwinner for the family, which had prevented her from coming to see him and from writing to him more often.

But now he could no longer blind himself to the real truth, which was that his wife and family no longer wanted him. They did not care what happened to him in the future as long as he did not bother them. And the pain of acceptance of those facts was all the deeper because of the hope which had preceded it.

For a moment he gave himself up to the dejection which filled him, then suddenly he remembered what his wife had said. They were not all against him. Kate had believed in him. She had written to him more than once, stilted scrappy little notes which he had treasured, and the thought of them brought him some small measure of comfort.

He lifted his head suddenly, disturbed by a noise outside the sitting room door, and heard a high clear voice say,

"Come on, James. The car's here. We'll be late if you don't get a move on."

"Surely that is the bride's privilege, my dear," a pedantic voice replied, a voice which Gregory had no difficulty in recognising.

It's Di, he thought, and James, and realised that his daughter was about to leave the house for her marriage to the young man who was a stranger to him. Of whom he had never heard until that day and whose name he still did not know.

"Not this bride," he heard Diane answer gaily. "I promised Neil faithfully I'd be dead on time, so come along, there's a pet."

So, my soon to be son-in-law is called Neil, Gregory thought, and as he moved across to the window he wondered if Diane had told him about her father. Whether he knew that her father existed even, except as a shadowy figure, the man who had deserted his family without reason.

Then he shrugged philosophically. If he did not know that his future father-in-law had been in gaol, it would not be long before he was told, and it would be Diane's problem to explain her lack of openness to him, if she could.

Because if he stayed, as he planned to do, everyone would know the real truth. There was no hope of hiding it in a village such as Beilton, and for the first time he understood the fear he had seen in Shelagh's eyes.

Almost he was tempted to pick up his case and raincoat and go away, quietly and secretly as he had come, but it was only a momentary impulse. Because he could not go not yet. Not without seeing once again his little Kate, without trying to make a new life for his family and for himself.

He stood well back in the shadow of

the curtains so that he would not be seen and watched his daughter come out of the house, her silky fair hair swinging against her shoulders, the bridal veil making a fairylike frame for her happy face.

He drew in his breath sharply, feeling the blood course hotly through him as he remembered that other wedding.

Almost he thought he was seeing Shelagh again, as she had looked when she came slowly down the aisle to where he waited at the altar, filled with love and pride for this girl who was entrusting herself to him.

Then Diane laughed up at James as she got into the car, and the picture splintered and was gone. Because dear as she had been to him and still was, he knew that Shelagh had never had the blazing confidence, the acceptance without question of whatever life might have to offer her in the future, which his tall daughter so obviously had.

He waited until the car drove away then turned and sat down, covering his face with his hands, giving himself up momentarily to the pain which stabbed through him. The pain of realising that he had come home, unlooked for and unwanted, without prospects and without a future, because he could not prove it was not he who had crashed into that other car, injuring the child in it then driving away without, as a doctor, stopping to do what he could to save a life.

Then he straightened his shoulders with a conscious effort. What was past was gone now and nothing he could do would alter it. He was on his own and it was up to him to make a new life for himself.

Suddenly, in spite of the pain of knowing that Diane did not want him at her wedding, he knew that he must see her married, this first born of his who had seemed to him so like a miracle when he had seen her, immediately after she was born. And on that impulse he went quickly out of the house and began to walk towards the village church, whose spire he could see dominating the roofs of the houses.

When he reached it he went in quietly and sat down in one of the rear pews, moving along it until he was partly hidden by a wide stone pillar. He was in time to hear Diane exchange her wedding vows with her bride-groom, but it was not until the bridal party came down the aisle later that he realised that the tall bridesmaid in the golden yellow dress with a saucy wreath of golden daisies on her brown hair was Kate.

He watched as she walked behind Diane and her new husband, thinking that although she had grown since he had last seen her, she had not really changed very much. She was still plump with the plumpness of youth, which even the cleverly cut dress she was wearing could not fully disguise.

As if drawn by his intent gaze she looked towards him and he dodged back behind the pillar, not wanting her to see him then in case it upset her, spoiled the day for her because he was there, the uninvited guest. So that he did not notice his wife stumble and almost fall as she caught sight of him, then grip Neil's father's arm more tightly as if it was a lifeline.

Someone else had seen him, too. A woman standing alone in a nearby pew had observed his quick withdrawal and looked at him curiously.

When the bridal party had left the church he knelt down and buried his face in his hands, in case anyone among the people who were now filing slowly out should recognise him.

And kneeling there, hearing the swelling sound of the organ, he gradually found a measure of the peace which until then had been denied to him.

When he left the church, blinking in the bright sunshine, the last of the guests were driving away, but as he turned to go back to Shelagh's house, a woman hesitating by a parked car said diffidently, with a smile,

"Are you going to the reception? Can I give you a lift?"

"No thank you," he said curtly. "I'm not a guest."

"Aren't you? I thought — " She hesitated, looking at him with a puzzled frown. "Haven't we met before?"

"No. I've never seen you in my life," he snapped, and strode away without a backward glance.

Though only he knew how difficult it was not to turn round when he came to a bend in the road, to go back and apologise to her for his response to her kindness, his churlish rejection of her proffered friendliness.

He had probably alienated her completely, he told himself grimly, he who could do with all the friends he could find now, to help to disperse the loneliness and despair which had been with him all that dreary time while he was in prison, and which had deepened and intensified in the short time he had been home.

Shelagh had still not recovered from the shock of seeing Gregory in the church as she stood between Neil and his father later, welcoming the guests to the wedding reception.

"Thank you. It's very kind of you," she said, over and over again, feeling as if she had been there for hours, shaking hands and murmuring conventional words of greeting through stiffly smiling lips.

It was a relief when at last Diane and Neil moved out of line to mingle with the guests, a relief all the greater because what she had feared had not happened. Gregory had not turned up at the hotel, to ruin Di's day for her, as she knew it would have done. And she felt a sharp pang of thankfulness because he had been big enough to resist the temptation to assuage his own hurt by striking savagely back at his family.

"Thank goodness that's over." Plump

36

Mrs. Carter, Neil's mother, heaved a sigh of relief. "My poor feet! I knew I should've worn my old shoes but pride wouldn't let me. It's been a lovely wedding, Mrs. Muir, and Di looks really beautiful. Eh, if your husband could see her now, he'd be that sorry he'd deserted you all."

Shelagh felt as if all the blood had drained away from her heart at those words, and if she made any reply, had no idea what it was. She was aware only of the knowledge that Mrs. Carter had unwittingly underlined the difficulty which faced her when people found out the deception she had practised.

As they inevitably would unless she could persuade Gregory to go away. At once. That very day. Before anybody saw and recognised him. Though how she was going to accomplish that she did not know.

Suddenly, more than anything else, she wanted to talk to James, to tell him her worries as she had done before, to receive from him the help and comfort which he had given to her so unstintingly over the past months.

She looked eagerly around and saw him at last, standing with a group of men and women whom Shelagh vaguely remembered as belonging to the same Golf Club as James, and moved quickly and purposefully towards him, hardly seeing any other people on her way.

"James," she said and grasped his arm tightly. "I've got to talk to you."

Calmly he finished what he was saying, then looked down coldly at her.

"Not now, Shelagh. I'm busy, as you can see. Later, my dear," he said, and removed his arm deliberately from her grasp, half turning away from her and continuing his conversation with his friends.

For a moment she stood there, hardly able to believe that James could snub her so cruelly, then as the hot colour rushed into her face she moved quickly away, blundering to the other side of the room, trying to control the trembling in her limbs, to make herself invisible to the people round about her until she had gained control over herself.

"Are you feeling all right, Mrs. Muir?"

She turned at the anxious question and saw with relief that it was Dorothy who had come up to her, the woman who ran the shop so successfully and who had designed the gowns for herself, Di and Kate. The one person whom she did not mind seeing her emotion.

"I've got a splitting headache, that's all, Dorothy."

"I'm not surprised, the way you've been driving yourself these last few weeks. Sit down, my dear, and I'll bring you a sherry."

"No, don't bother. It's time for the wedding breakfast," she said, as the double doors at the end of the room were opened. "I'm just hungry. I expect. There wasn't time to eat properly this morning."

But when she sat down at the table, between Neil's father and another man whom she did not know, she only toyed with the food which was served to her.

She listened to the speeches, laughed in the right places, applauded the telegrams and the cutting of the wedding cake, and talked to the men on either side of her, but all without really knowing what was happening.

When the time came for Neil and Diane to change before going away on their honeymoon she roused herself to see them off happily, so that her daughter would not be worried.

"Bye, Mom. See you in a fortnight." Diane kissed her lovingly. "Take care of yourself and thanks for everything."

And as the car moved off, coloured balloons floating behind it, she knew she had succeeded, even though the effort had left her feeling completely exhausted.

"Ah, there you are, Shelagh."

She turned at James's genial words, looking at him defensively, before realising after a moment that he was completely ignoring or had really forgotten the snub he had administered to her earlier.

"Ready to go home now?"

She hesitated, knowing that she ought not to allow him to treat her in such a fashion but feeling too weary and sick at heart to do anything about it.

"Yes. Have you seen Kate and Brian?"

"They've gone to the car already." He smiled down at her, putting his hand under her elbow. "Come along, Shelagh. You look worn out, my dear."

She blinked back the tears which rushed into her eyes at the kindness in his voice. This was the James she knew, not the cold voiced man who had looked at her as if she were a stranger, and she felt a surge of relief that she had not, after all, been mistaken in him.

"It's been a tiring day," she said. "I'll be glad to get home."

But as she went with him to the car she knew how untrue that was. There was nothing she wanted less than to have to face up to telling James and Brian and Kate that Gregory had come home, as she must do within the next half hour.

When they stopped in front of the house it was an effort to ask him to come in, and she was deeply thankful when he said,

"Not now, Shelagh. I'll come along later, perhaps, if I may."

"Just as you like," she answered, glad of the short respite, even though it only postponed the moment when she would inevitably have to tell him about Gregory.

As they turned to go into the house Kate said crossly,

"Why didn't you put him off, Mom? We don't want him tonight."

"I couldn't do that, dear. Not after" She stopped, looking at her son and daughter, searching for the right words with which to break the news to them.

"Brian! Kate! There's something I've got to tell you before we go in."

They looked at her, Brian's eyes surprised but she saw in Kate's an expression almost of fear, as if something she dreaded was about to happen.

"Mom, it isn't — you're not — " she began.

Shelagh did not pretend to misunderstand her.

"No. It's — your father's come home."

She saw the fear fade from Kate's eyes to be replaced by a blazing happiness.

"Dad? I can't believe it. When did he come? Mom, isn't that just fab?"

"Fab! That's the last thing I'd call it." Brian's voice was angry, an anger which to Shelagh's ears held a distinct note of fear. "He hasn't come to stay, has he?"

"Why shouldn't he?" Kate asked militantly.

"Because he ought to have enough decency to keep away, that's why. He's done us enough harm."

"Brian, don't," Shelagh said urgently.

"Why not? D'you think I want everyone to know my father's a gaol bird? Bad enough when all the fellows at school knew about it."

"Stop it, Brian." Even to her own ears Shelagh's voice sounded tense and hoarse and she knew that because of the worries of that day she was not being very diplomatic in her handling of her son. "He's here for tonight at least, so behave yourself when you meet him."

"I'm not going to. I'm going straight out again as soon as I've changed, and if he isn't gone by the time I get back, I'll be the one who leaves home."

Shelagh watched him run up the stairs and knew that the life she had built up so laboriously for them all was disintegrating around her, and she could do nothing to stop it.

She hardly heard Kate's angry reply, hurled after her brother's retreating back, as she went wearily into the sitting room.

She only realised Gregory had come in when Kate said joyously,

"Dad! Gee, I'm glad to see you."

"Kate, my little Kate." He hugged her tightly, then held her away from him, his eyes tender. "Though you're not so little now, are you?" Then the teasing note went out of his voice and he said, urgently, "No, don't cry, poppet."

"I'm not, Dad, or at least only a bit, because I'm so happy."

He laughed then and his arm tightened around her lovingly. Shelagh watched them, seeing with a pang of sadness the light in his eyes, knowing with a strange and unexpected feeling of regret that the days had gone when she had been the one who had brought that look to his face.

"So am I, pet. Thank you for writing to me."

"That's all right," she said gruffly, then looked at him anxiously. "You won't go away again, Dad?"

"No." Over her head he looked

challengingly at Shelagh. "I'm going to stay here with you all."

"That's great. Isn't it, Mummy?"

"Yes, dear." Shelagh pulled off her hat, pushing the thick brown hair off her hot forehead. "Could you make some tea for us, Kate?"

"Yes, of course, Mom."

"Change your dress first, though."

"Rightho. Shan't be a jiff."

There was silence when she had gone, then Gregory said quietly, "Well, Shelagh?"

She sighed sharply.

"I don't know what to say, Gregory."

He sat down beside her on the sofa and put his hand over hers.

"You're tired out. Forget it for tonight. There's always tomorrow."

"I can't." Her hand moved restlessly under his. "Brian says he'll leave home if you stay."

His lips tightened.

"Then he'll have to go, won't he?"

"How can he? He's not twenty yet."

"Old enough not to go round making

stupid threats when he's no intention of carrying them out."

"How do you know that? He isn't easy to control, Gregory. You'll understand better when you see him — "

He laughed.

"With it, is he? Well, we all go through that stage when we have to be in the fashion or die! Nothing wrong with that."

"But it isn't only that. Brian — he's been difficult, self-willed. I'm afraid for him — "

His hand tightened on hers.

"You can't shelter them all their lives, Shelagh," he said quietly. "They've got to learn to grow up some time, to stand on their own feet. To leave you, as Di has done, and blaze a trail for themselves."

She pulled her hand away from his, fear for the future making her voice unsteady.

"You don't care, do you, as long as you're all right."

"You're forgetting something, aren't

you?" His voice was hard and cold, all the warmth and gentleness gone from it as though they had never been. "Brian's my son as well as yours. Just as this house is my home, bought with my money," he added deliberately.

She flushed and got up quickly.

"All right then, stay! And take the consequences."

"And they are?"

"I've told you that."

He looked at her without answering and she hurried into speech again, impelled by the tension which had been steadily increasing within her.

"Our marriage is over, Gregory. Don't forget that."

"I won't," he said quietly, and she felt a surge of relief because he had accepted the fact that she no longer wanted him as a husband. Though under that feeling there was another emotion which she did not then try to interpret.

She turned away and went towards the door.

"I'll take you up to your room now, before Kate comes back."

He picked up his raincoat and case and followed her upstairs, and as she walked in front of him she felt tension like a tightly rolled ball growing within her.

She stopped at last and pushed open a door at the end of the landing.

"This is it."

He went past her and put down his bag, looking around him without interest.

"I see. And where's your room?"

She stiffened, wondering if she had been mistaken in thinking he had understood her, after all.

"I've told you," she said quickly. "That's no concern of yours now."

He smiled grimly.

"You misunderstand me, Shelagh. I only want to know so I don't go in by mistake."

She coloured at his sardonic words.

"Oh, you make me tired. If you must know, it's here."

She walked to the other end of the landing and opened a door there. He looked past her into the prettily furnished room with its single bed, but said nothing.

Then as she closed the door decisively he put his fingers under her chin, forcing her to look up at him.

"Back to single blessedness, eh, Shelagh? Well, remember what I told you. If you ever change your mind, you'll have to come to me, because I will never come to you again."

She was aware of a pulse beating heavily in her throat against his fingers, but when she answered him her voice was strong and steady.

"I won't change my mind, ever Gregory."

He looked down at her silently, then released her with an almost contemptuous gesture, before walking away as if she no longer existed.

She waited until he disappeared around the bend in the staircase before she followed him, watching from the top of the stairs as he went into the sitting room without once looking back. Then she went wearily up the next flight of stairs to Brian's room, which was at the top of the house.

She knocked and waited nervously for a reply, then when she heard no sound at all, she opened the door slowly and looked in. There was no one there. Only the suit he had worn for the wedding was flung carelessly over a chair, and she knew she was too late. He had already gone and now she could only wait until he returned, as he must surely do, before she could talk to him again, try to make him see reason.

She sat down on the bed, facing up to the knowledge that however difficult that day had been, her troubles were only just beginning.

Gregory had accused her of tying the children to her apron strings, but she knew that wasn't really true. Only she knew how real her worry about Brian had been, especially during those first

51

months of his father's imprisonment. Suppose his return started it all off again, just when she thought he was settling down?

"I can't bear it if it does," she said aloud, then got up quickly, startled by the sound of her own voice, aware now of a feeling of complete mental and physical exhaustion, instead of the happiness she should have been experiencing. The happiness of knowing that her daughter had married the man she loved and that she had found the courage to tell Gregory that she no longer wanted him as a husband, with none of the argument and distress that she had expected would follow that difficult task.

He had accepted the ending of their life together so quietly and easily. Too easily, she thought suddenly, and wondered, for the first time, whether he too had been glad to make an end of their marriage.

But instead of that thought bringing with it relief, because if it was true, then

52

she need not fear that he had been hurt badly, she felt only an intensification of the exhaustion which was making it difficult for her to think and plan as she knew she must do, for all their sakes.

3

"TEA up, Mom! Come and get it!"

"Coming," Shelagh answered Kate's call, glad to be roused from her disquieting thoughts.

"I've put yours on the little table by the fire," her daughter said cheerfully when she went into the sitting room.

"Thank you, dear."

She sat down, listening to Gregory and Kate talking, answering if they spoke to her, but gradually beginning to feel as if she was a stranger in her own home, entirely superfluous to the well-being and happiness of either of them. It was a relief when she felt able to get up and leave them alone together.

Gregory looked up as she moved.

"Finished already, Shelagh?"

"Yes. It's time I was thinking about a meal — "

"Oh, bother! Old James is coming, isn't he?" Kate grumbled.

Shelagh's lips tightened.

"Kate, I've warned you — "

"Sorry, Mom, but I can't help it if I wish he wasn't, can I?"

Gregory smiled.

"Don't you like him, poppet?"

"No, I don't — "

"Kate, I won't tell you again," Shelagh said, then as she saw the mulish look on her daughter's face, added more gently, "Please, dear. I can't stand a scene tonight."

"Sorry, Mom. I didn't mean to upset you. I'll be a perfect angel to him."

"That would be a miracle, and it'd frighten him away completely, I should think. Just be friendly and pleasant to him, Kate. That's all I ask."

Gregory looked at her with sudden awareness.

"You're tired out, Shelagh, not really fit to do any entertaining. Would you like me to ring him and put him off?"

Almost she was tempted to let him do as he suggested, so that it would be he who would break the news of his arrival to James, but it was only a momentary desire.

She knew she could not do it. That it would not be fair to treat James so badly when he had done so much for her, for them all. The least she could do in return was to tell him herself so that only she would be a witness to his inevitable reaction.

"No, thank you," she said at last. "I'll be all right when I've had a bath and changed."

"As you please, though I think it's a pity —"

She looked at him quickly, visited by a sudden suspicion, and after a moment said hesitantly,

"Perhaps you'd rather — I'll understand if you don't feel like meeting him, Gregory."

"Good idea!" Kate's voice was enthusiastic. "We'll neither of us meet him, Dad. Let's have our supper in the kitchen, by ourselves."

He laughed, shaking his head.

"Not likely! I'm looking forward to seeing James again. I want to prove something to myself. I'll tell you what, though, Kate. We could go for a walk and stretch our legs while your mother's getting the meal ready. That's if you don't want us to help, Shelagh."

"No, there's nothing much to be done. You go if you want to."

She watched from the landing window as they walked down the path together, her young daughter and the man whom she had once loved, and for the first time realised, with a sense of shock, how changed he was.

The broad, strong shoulders were slightly stooped and the suit, the same one he had worn when he went away, hung on him as if he had lost a lot of weight.

She went slowly into her bedroom, beginning to understand for the first time how much he had suffered over the past months. How much he would

57

still have to suffer in the years which lay before him, deprived as he would be of the right to practise the profession which he loved.

They had still not come back when James arrived, which meant that she was able to tell him quietly about Gregory's return with nobody else present.

He stared at her disbelievingly.

"Gregory? Here?"

"Yes."

"And you've let him stay?"

"I had to. He's got nowhere else to go. And as he reminded me, this is his house, bought with his money — "

"Did he?" James said grimly. "I'll soon put him right about that!"

She took told of his arm urgently.

"No, please. Don't say anything to him, not yet. You'll only make things worse."

"That's nonsense, Shelagh"

"It isn't. He and Diane — they're alike. The more you oppose them, the more obstinate they become."

His fingers closed over hers.

"And that's the kind of man you're married to. It doesn't bear thinking about. Shelagh, if you'd only do what I've asked you to."

"No. I've told you before — "

She pulled her hand away from his, aware of a strong reluctance to talk about this desire of his, that she should ask Gregory for her freedom so that she and James could marry.

Even while he was away, she had never wanted to discuss it. Now, when he was only just home again, it was the very last thing she wanted either to think or to talk about.

James looked at her out of hurt, blue eyes.

"I can't understand you, Shelagh," he said huffily, "but if that's what you want, then I suppose I've got to agree."

"It's what I must want. Don't you see, dear, it wouldn't be wise, especially now. Everybody thinks he deserted us, remember, so we've got to pretend we're all glad he's come back. That way nobody need ever know the real truth."

"You're talking nonsense," he said impatiently. "Surely even you can't be as naïve as to believe that?"

She coloured, annoyance rising in her at his derisive words.

"Why not?"

"Because Gregory will have to report to the police. How long do you think it will take for that to get around in a place this size?"

She stared at him, her eyes dark with dismay, everything else forgotten in the fear his words had brought.

"That isn't true!" she said at last.

"Of course it is. Didn't he tell you?"

"No."

"Then he should have done, and I don't mind telling him so. Where is he?"

"He's out with Kate. James, when they come in — don't say anything, please. Leave it to me — "

60

"Oh, very well. I'm beginning to think it's a pity I came at all tonight. In fact, if I'd known he was here, I don't think I would have. I think I'd better leave."

"I'm sorry," Shelagh began, then stopped, shaken by a surge of deep anger.

Why should she apologise to him for something which was not her fault, she thought resentfully, and said aloud, coldly,

"You must do as you want to."

But when he had gone, walking down the path, his back stiff with resentment, she was sorry she had been so sharp with him. Because it was not really his fault that he had been the one to destroy all her hopes of hiding the truth from their friends.

Gregory was to blame for that, as he was for everything else, and by the time he and Kate came back, so evidently very happy together, all the anger she felt had been directed against him.

"Why didn't you tell me you'd have

to report to the police?" she demanded, as soon as he walked in.

He stopped, looking at her frowningly. "Who told you that?"

"James. Is it true?"

"Yes."

"You might have told me, instead of letting me hear about it from him."

"I intended to, at the right time, but I thought you'd had enough shocks for one day. It's a pity James had to be so busy," he added grimly. "Where is he?"

"He's gone."

"Just as well, too. I'd have told him a thing or two if he'd been here. In fact, I've a good mind to ring him now and let him know exactly what I think of him."

"No, don't do that!" she said quickly, and wondered wryly if she was fated to be always trying to keep the peace between these two so different men in her life. "There's no harm done. I had to know some time. Come and have your supper. You must be hungry." But

62

although she had hardly eaten anything herself that day, every mouthful was so difficult to swallow that in the end she did not even pretend she was hungry.

When the meal was over Gregory said quietly,

"You go and sit down, Shelagh. Kate and I will wash the dishes."

"All right," she answered, though she would have preferred to keep busy rather than to sit and worry about the future, as she knew she would do.

When they eventually joined her, laughing together at something which had amused them, she got up abruptly.

"I'm tired. I'm going to bed now. And don't you be too late, Kate. It's school tomorrow, remember."

"I won't, Mom. Goodnight. God bless," Kate said.

"Goodnight, Shelagh. Sleep well."

Gregory's quiet words followed her as she went up stairs, and although she knew she had little hope of sleeping that night, at least before Brian was safely home again, she found them curiously comforting and soothing.

It was an effort to undress, and when she had put on her dressing gown she sat down in the easy chair to wait for her son to come in, as she knew he must do because he had to go back to University the next day.

Through the veil of tiredness which wrapped her around like an almost tangible thing, she heard Kate come upstairs, followed very soon by Gregory, and then the house became quiet.

It seemed only a few minutes later when she sat up with a start, hearing Gregory's voice saying sharply,

"Who's down there?"

She looked at her watch, seeing with complete surprise that it was a quarter past two. And as she went quickly to the door she realised that in spite of all that had happened to disturb her that day, she must have fallen asleep.

She went quietly along the landing to the head of the stairs and looked down into the lighted hall, seeing with dismay that Brian was standing defensively just inside the front door.

Gregory's voice was quiet but there was a grim note in it which Shelagh heard with a feeling of near panic, a feeling which deepened when Brian said belligerently,

"What's that got to do with you? I don't have to give you an account of what I've been doing. I'm not a child any longer, you know."

"Then why act like one? How dare you worry your mother with your stupid dramatics?"

She heard Brian mutter an answer, and although she could not make out his words, Gregory's reply made them clear to her.

"If you think that's true, then shouldn't it make you even more careful not to hurt her? Now, get off to bed and remember in future that you're grown up, and act accordingly."

His voice was like a whiplash and Shelagh clenched her hands tightly together, waiting for the clash which she was sure must be inevitable. But it did not come. Brian stood for a moment looking defiantly at his father, then lurched past him towards the stairs.

She moved then, hurrying back to her bedroom, anxious not to let them know that she had witnessed that encounter, and feeling weak with relief at Brian's capitulation.

It was only when she had closed the door behind her that she suddenly realised that Gregory had still been fully dressed, and when she lay down gratefully in her bed it was this thought which stayed in her mind. But before she could puzzle out all its implications, she fell suddenly and deeply asleep.

It was later than usual when she awoke next morning. She got up and pulled on her dressing gown, then went quickly along the landing to call Kate and Brian.

It was only when she was returning that she noticed Gregory's bedroom door standing wide open. She stopped and looked inside, seeing with surprise that the bed was neatly made, as if it had not been slept in, and there seemed to be nothing belonging to him lying about.

And in that moment she thought she had found the answer to the puzzle which had worried her earlier. Gregory had still been fully dressed at two o'clock, had been awake and on his way downstairs when Brian came in, because he had been going away. He had been leaving as she had asked him to, slipping out of the house quietly, without saying goodbye to anyone.

She felt relief surge through her at this unexpected and easy end to all her worries, a relief which had in it a deep gratitude because he had been big enough to sink his own wishes in hers.

Then, as she pushed open the kitchen door it was all gone, lost in a blaze of irrational anger when he looked up from the newspaper he was reading.

"Good-morning, Shelagh," he said casually.

She took a deep breath, trying to control the choking feeling in her throat which was making it difficult for her to speak.

"What are you doing up so early? I thought when I saw your bedroom empty — the bed made — "

He grinned.

"You thought I'd gone? I'm afraid not. It's just that we old lags are used to early rising, and habits are hard to break. Just as we're used to making our beds and tidying our rooms."

"Oh, you — "

She turned away and went over to the stove, feeling the colour burn into her cheeks at his sardonic answer. The silence between them lengthened, broken only by the rustle of the newspaper as he turned the pages, until at last she could bear it no longer and said loudly,

"What do you want for breakfast?"

He looked up at her.

"I've had mine, thanks, and taken a cup of tea to Kate. I'd have brought

68

you one, too, if you hadn't put your bedroom out of bounds."

She turned back to the stove, clattering the pans unnecessarily, annoyed with herself because she had spoken to him and given him the opportunity once again to make her feel small.

"I never take tea in bed," she said shortly.

He laughed then.

"You've got a short memory, Shelagh. Many's the time I've made tea for us both and brought it back to bed." He paused, then when she did not answer, added deliberately. "Sorry. I didn't mean to remind you of those days."

For a moment she could not reply, then she said breathlessly,

"What are you planning to do today?"

He did not answer and she turned to look at him, puzzled by his lack of response, to find him regarding her with an expression which brought the blood rushing to her face again.

Slowly he got to his feet and came round the table to her, and she backed away until she was brought up short by the stove.

"You know, Shelagh," he said softly, "you're still quite something. No one would ever think you were the mother of three grown up children."

She swallowed convulsively and her hands went up to the lapels of her dressing gown, drawing them together, closing the deep gap which had appeared there, aware of an intensity of desire which made her tremble helplessly. A desire which, she suddenly knew, had roused within her an answering passion, a passion which was betraying all she had told this man, all she had promised herself.

"Never mind that!" she said, finding it an effort to speak because of the thudding of her heart in her throat. "I asked you what your plans are."

For a moment longer he held her glance with his, so that she felt all her resolution and strength ebbing away, then as abruptly as he had moved, he went away again, sitting down at the table and picking up the newspaper he had thrown down such a short time before.

"So you did," he said calmly. "Well, first I'll have to go to the police station."

She let her breath go on a sigh of relief and turned to the stove, holding on to it as she tried to still the emotion which his nearness had roused in her.

"And then?" she said at last.

He shrugged.

"I don't know. I haven't thought about it yet. This seems a very pretty part of the world, though. I'd like to do some exploring."

"Will you — you'll be looking for a job?"

He laughed shortly.

"Doing what? Who's going to employ me?"

She hesitated, then said reluctantly,

"You could come to the shop. I

suppose we could find something for you to do there."

He looked at her and she knew he had recognised the lack of enthusiasm behind her offer.

"And ruin your business? No, thanks. Anyway, I'm going to take a holiday. Enjoy my freedom after being cooped up for so many months in gaol." Then as he saw her make an impatient movement he added, caustically, "But not to worry, Shelagh. I won't be a burden on you. I'll sign on at the Employment Exchange today and make sure of my dole. I'm entitled to that. We learn all the dodges in prison, you know."

She shivered suddenly, uncontrollably, hearing a note in his voice which was so foreign to the Gregory she had known and loved that for a moment everything was lost in a wave of nostalgic pain which took her by surprise. As though it mattered to her now that he had become so changed, so hard and cynical.

Silently she finished cooking the breakfast, then went to call Brian and Kate again.

When she returned he said abruptly, "I'm going out now."

"Already? When will you be home?"

His face darkened.

"What do you want to know that for? You don't care what I do. You've made that pretty clear since I came back."

She was so taken aback by the unguarded pain in his eyes that she could not answer him immediately. Then it was too late as the door banged behind him.

She stood looking at it, her hands clasped tightly together, shaken again by the unexpected surge of passion within her, as she had been when Gregory had come close to her before.

She shivered, fighting to control that urge, recognising it for what it was, a desire for the love of which she had been deprived for so long. Desire which had been roused by her husband's nearness but which she knew had its roots not in love for him, but in the need for satisfaction of one of nature's strongest urges.

Gregory had been right when he had accused her of not caring what he did now. How could she when every feeling she had ever had for him was dead? Nevertheless, she was more shaken by his words than she had expected to be.

She turned quickly and walked back to the stove as she heard Kate come running down the stairs, trying to regain the peace of mind which she had gained so painfully over the past months, and which his coming had destroyed in a moment.

And as she automatically turned the bacon cooking under the grill she knew that before her were only turmoil and frustration, and a disruption of all their lives, while Gregory remained in Beilton.

4

THE same thoughts were in Gregory's mind as he stood outside the kitchen door, hearing the echo of its bang, sorry now that he had been so irritable with Shelagh.

It was not her fault, he admitted, as he began to walk towards the village. He ought to make allowances for the shock of his sudden return. Yet his own disappointment was so great that it was difficult for him to feel anything but resentment. Only somebody who was a complete saint could have felt otherwise, and, he thought grimly, no one could ever have described him as that.

It was quite a way to the police station, and by the time he reached it he had managed to shake off the effects of his clash with Shelagh.

He hesitated outside, loth to carry

out this necessary duty which seemed to set him apart from his fellow men even more than his prison sentence had done, and it took all his will power to force himself to go inside.

The constable on duty looked up as he hesitated in the doorway.

"Come in, sir. What can I do for you?" he asked pleasantly, but when Gregory told him his attitude changed at once.

"So you've come to report, have you? Just out of gaol. It's people like you who give us all our work," he grumbled. "Let's have the details then, and I don't want any of your lies."

"I've no intention of telling you lies — "

"Don't give me that injured innocent stuff. I know you old lags too well. You're all the same. Out for what you can get — "

"Who the devil do you think you're talking to?" Gregory interrupted furiously. "I'd like to knock you down, you young, jumped up — "

"Here, what's all this?"

A door at the other side of the room had opened and a burly man came in. The constable got up quickly.

"This man's just come out of gaol, Sergeant, and he's reporting as per instructions."

"And getting insulted for my pains," Gregory cut in.

"I don't want any of your lip"

"That's enough, Constable." The Sergeant's voice was firm and authoritative. "I'll attend to this. Come in here, sir, will you?"

Gregory followed him into the other room, feeling so humiliated by the reception given to him by the constable who was young enough to be his son, that he had to thrust his hands deep within his pockets to still their trembling.

"Sit down, sir. Now let me have all the particulars."

Gregory gave them to him, the effort of doing so helping him to control the emotion which had been roused in him.

"I apologise for my young constable," the Sergeant said when he had written down all he had been told. "He's full of enthusiasm and zeal, and youth is something he'll recover from as the years pass."

"I suppose I shouldn't have let him irritate me. I'll have to learn to take that kind of thing."

"People have short memories, sir."

"I hope you're right, but I'm not convinced."

The Sergeant looked at him out of shrewd blue eyes.

"Can I give you a word of advice, sir?"

"Of course."

"Then I'd say, hold your head high and keep that temper of yours under control, even if people do treat you like my constable did. And remember this. I'm your friend, not your enemy, just as long as you behave yourself and keep your nose clean."

Gregory smiled wryly.

"Thanks, Sergeant. I'll try to do that."

"Good. Now take this along to the Employment Exchange and sign on. You'll be wanting a job, I take it?"

"Yes, though I don't know what at. My training didn't fit me for anything but being a doctor, and I'm not allowed to do that any longer," he finished bitterly.

The Sergeant gripped his shoulder reassuringly.

"Maybe not, but there's always jobs for those who want to work."

"For me, at forty-five, with a prison record? It's not the best of references, is it?" and as he left the police station he was shaken by a feeling of despair which was increased by the necessity of giving particulars about himself to the young clerk at the Employment Exchange.

"It's not going to be easy to place you," he said, making no secret of his opinion of the man who had spent the last few months in gaol and had also been struck off the Medical Register.

"That's your problem, not mine,"

Gregory snapped, and flung out of the office before he lost his temper again.

He hesitated in the street outside, then began to walk towards the moors which rose to the west of the town. striding along so lost in his own bitter thoughts that he did not notice who he was passing. Gradually, however, the quiet of the countryside brought him a measure of peace, and he began to enjoy the walk.

He was striding past a high hedge which cut off the fields from the lane when he first heard the sound and stopped to listen. It came again, a whimper followed by a sharp yelping which seemed to come from the other side of the bushes.

There was no way through for a man and he hurried on until he came to a gate, securely padlocked and guarded by strands of barbed wire.

He climbed it gingerly, then went back the way he had come, feeling a sick anger when he finally saw the dog, a young golden retriever caught on a piece of the barbed wire which was threaded through the hedge.

He knelt down and examined her without touching her, seeing how her struggles to release herself had resulted only in the barbs biting in more deeply, leaving jagged wounds in her flank.

"Good girl. Stay still now," he said soothingly, and wished he had thick gloves with him, knowing that in her pain she might bite the hands which were trying to help her.

She wagged her tail feebly and as he bent over her, still talking quietly, he pulled off his tie and made it into a noose, catching the dog's muzzle in it and tying her jaws gently together.

When the last wicked barb came away he lifted her in his arms and looked at the name plate on her collar.

"Black, Deepden Farm," he read aloud and wished he had a greater knowledge of the district. All he could do was to start walking back to the village in the hope that he would find a vet there.

He went quickly back the way he had come and was relieved after a while to hear the sound of a car engine. He stopped and held up his hand as a Land-rover came slowly towards him.

It pulled up with a screech of brakes and the driver got out quickly and came towards him. It was the woman who had spoken to him at Diane's wedding.

He thought she had recognised him, too, but she was too concerned about the dog to do anything but say, with sharp anxiety,

"It's Jill. What's happened to her?"

"Is she your dog?"

"Yes. I've been searching for her all over the place. She got out and she's too young to be without a lead." She caressed the dog's head lovingly. "What's wrong with you, my beauty?"

"She got mixed up with some barbed wire, I'm afraid."

Her hazel eyes darkened with anger. "That man again! I've told him before about putting wire in the hedges, but he doesn't take any notice."

"I think she should be taken to a vet right away."

"Yes, of course. I'll do that."

She turned towards the Land-rover and he followed her, putting the dog gently on the passenger seat.

"Oh, your tie," she said and began to undo it.

He put his hand over hers.

"No, leave it. She's still in pain and may bite."

"Not me! She's my dog."

He smiled.

"I know, but better leave it for now. Maybe I can call and collect it sometime and see how Jill is going on — Miss Black?"

"Mrs. Black," she corrected. "And please do call. Deepden Farm. Anyone will tell you. Can I take you anywhere?" she added, as she switched on the engine.

"No, thanks. I'm out walking."

He stood back and watched her drive away, surprised at the disappointment he had felt when she had said she was Mrs. Black. As if it mattered to him whether she was married or not, he thought as he walked along, this woman who had the kindest eyes he had seen for a very long time.

He was on his way home when he suddenly realised he was hungry and went into the next public house for something to eat and drink.

He asked for a Ploughman's lunch, amused by the name and looking with approval at the man sized sandwich of cheese and the foaming tankard of beer which the barmaid planted in front of him. He was glad when she did not go away immediately, but stayed to talk to him in a friendly way while he ate.

"I enjoyed that," he said at last, draining the last drops from the tankard.

"It's hard to beat, so it is," the woman said. "Pleased to have met you, sir. Come in again, won't you."

He continued on his way, feeling at peace with himself and the world.

He had met two friendly people that day, three if he counted the police sergeant, and their friendliness had given him back some of the self respect he had lost.

It was late afternoon when he reached home and Shelagh came into the hall when she heard him.

"Where on earth have you been?" she asked sharply.

"Walking."

"All this time? I expected you back for lunch."

"You did? I didn't think you'd have cared whether I came or not," he said briefly.

She bit her lips hard, to stop herself from making the bitter reply which leaped into her mind.

"You might have let me know."

"I'm sorry. I will next time." He hesitated, then asked abruptly, "Do you know a Mrs. Black? From Deepen Farm?"

She stared at him, surprised by his unexpected question.

85

"Marion Black, do you mean?"

"Probably."

"Of course I do. Why?"

"I met her while I was out. Where's her farm?"

"It's on the Sawdon Road. Why?" she asked again.

He shrugged.

"Oh, no reason," he said, but as he went upstairs to his room he knew she was looking after him, puzzled by the questions which he had asked so casually, but which she knew were important to him.

Long before morning came he had made up his mind that he would take Marion Black at her word and call on her that day, admitting to himself that he wanted to see the woman with the friendly eyes again.

He waited until Shelagh had left for the shop then set out, breathing deeply, enjoying his freedom after so many months incarceration.

That had been the thing he had found hardest to bear, the fact that he could not come and go as he wanted to. And that was very odd, he told himself wryly as he tramped along, hardly noticing that he was going uphill steadily, because nobody could be more tied than the average doctor in general practice without an assistant.

But that was a forbidden thought and he thrust it out of his mind, determined not to give way to self pity because he was no longer allowed to do the job he loved.

When he came to the inn where he had lunched the previous day he went in. The same barmaid was on duty and he greeted her cheerfully, but this time she hardly spoke to him, only serving him quickly and turning away without any of the friendliness she had shown him before.

He drank his beer and went out, filled once again with the old depression, annoyed with himself because he had not had the courage to ask her what was wrong. Though he would have been wasting his time, because he knew the answer.

She had heard what was probably common knowledge in the village now — that he had just been let out of prison — and had given him the kind of reception which he must expect in the future.

He breasted a short rise and stopped, looking across the valley, seeing the fields and trees in their autumn dress spread out before him. A little way off he saw the farmhouse, built squarely against the hillside, looking dependable and friendly, rather like Marion Black herself, he thought suddenly.

He walked towards it along a drive which descended quite steeply, but as he neared the house his pace slowed. What if she, too, had heard about him? Might he see the friendliness gone from her eyes, as it had from the barmaid's?

He was almost on the point of turning back when a red-gold bombshell with a girdle of white around her, rocketed up to him and pawed at his legs, her bright eyes beaming.

"So you recognised me? Clever girl!" He bent down, gently fondling the dog's ears. "No need to ask if you're all right."

"No, none at all."

He straightened quickly at the words, the smile dying on his lips to be replaced by a wary expression as he recognised the knowledge in Marion's eyes. And in that moment he was sure that once she had given him back his tie she would not want to see him again.

Then he became aware that she was still smiling at him, that her eyes were just as friendly as they had been yesterday.

"She really is clever," she said, and bent down to pick the dog up. "She saw you before I did and recognised you. Won't you come in, Mr. Muir, and have some coffee?"

He hesitated.

"You know who I am?"

"Yes. When I saw you outside church I thought — then yesterday I was sure. Kate's very like you, you know. Too like for anybody to mistake the relationship."

"Thank you," he said simply, feeling absurdly pleased by her words. "But I think I ought to tell you — "

"That you've been in prison? There's no need to. I know it already. I also know that Kate won't believe you did anything wrong, and I have great faith in her judgement."

"Thank you," he said again, with difficulty.

"And now, what about that coffee?"

"If you don't think it unwise."

"Why? Because people may talk?" She led the way into a big sunny kitchen. "I'm used to that and I never let it worry me. Here, take Jill, will you? It's no use putting her back in her basket. She'll only come out again to you." She smiled at him mischievously. "Dogs have excellent judgement, too. Don't you agree?"

He stroked the dog's ears gently as she turned towards the stove, thinking what a very kind person she was. Big in every way, mentally as well as physically. Yet as she poured out the coffee and gave it to him, there was an economy and neatness, a lightness about her movements that belied her size.

"Thank you." He took the coffee cup from her. "Why did you say you're used to people talking? Don't answer that, Mrs. Black," he added quickly. "I've no right to pry into your affairs."

"Of course I'll answer it. Why not? And please call me Marion."

"I'd like to, Marion," he said and was surprised at the pleasure it gave him to say her name.

"People talked because I was thirty-seven when I married and John, my husband, was sixty-five. I was his second wife."

"Widowers very often marry again. Nothing strange about that, Marion."

"No, only they said I'd married him as a last hope, but it wasn't true. He was a wonderful man and I loved him. We only had seven years together but they were very happy ones for me, for both of us." She was silent for a moment. "It hurt at first, you know, especially as I'd always been an ugly duckling, but I soon learned to take no notice. You will, too, you know."

"Maybe, though as you're wrong about one thing, you could be wrong about the other," he said coolly.

"What do you mean?"

"That whatever you are, you're not an ugly duckling. You're a very fine woman, Marion."

She flushed faintly, though her eyes glinted at him mockingly.

"Thank you, kind sir, though I should tell you that flattery will get you nowhere!"

"It wasn't flattery. And you have other talents, too. Do you run the farm singlehanded?"

"No. I have a cowman and a pigman,

as well as a shepherd. I also employ a farm manager, though the last one left recently and I haven't managed to replace him yet. Are you looking for a job?"

"Me? I know nothing about farming."

She shrugged.

"You don't need to know an awful lot — about the technical side, I mean. I can take care of that. That's why the manager left."

"But even so —"

"Look," she interrupted. "I'm not offering you an easy position, you know. You'd have to work hard and do as you were told up to a point, at least until you knew your way about. I'd teach you the job myself, but I can assure you that if you didn't come up to standard in a reasonable time, I'd have no compunction in asking you to go."

"There's no sense in it!"

"I don't agree. I keep a pedigree herd of cows, as well as pigs and sheep. You're a doctor. You can't practise any longer among people, so wouldn't animals be the next best thing?" she asked deliberately.

His lips tightened.

"Yes, but it wouldn't work. It wouldn't be fair to you."

"Because people might talk? I've told you, I don't care about that."

"Then I must, for you. The other thing is that I'm not ready to take a job yet. Can you understand that?"

She smiled warmly.

"Easily, Gregory, but if you change your mind will you come and tell me? Promise?"

"Yes, I promise. And thank you, Marion, for — well, for everything."

"I haven't done anything," she began, then turned as the door was pushed open. "Yes, Sam? What is it?"

"You'd better come, mistress. Yon Ministry chap's arrived and wants to see you."

"All right. Tell him I won't be a minute," she said brusquely.

Gregory got to his feet, putting Jill

down gently onto the floor.

"I'll go then, Marion."

She held out her hand.

"Come again. Any time you feel like it."

He took her hand in his briefly, finding her strong clasp and parting words oddly comforting.

"Thank you, I will. Bye for now," he said, and went with her out into the yard.

When he reached the top of the road leading from the farmhouse he turned and looked back. She was still standing where he had left her and he raised his hand in farewell, watching until she was out of sight around the side of the house before setting out on the long walk home.

Though he did not notice the length, perhaps because of the warmth which seemed to wrap him around, engendered by the thought that for the first time somebody had told him he was needed.

And although he knew he could

not take advantage of her kindness, nevertheless it was very precious to know that she had offered him a job spontaneously, as if she meant it. Not as Shelagh had done, grudgingly, half hoping he would refuse. And as he tramped along, he found he was whistling to himself, a thing he had not done for a very long time.

5

SHELAGH was standing by the stove stirring the gravy for their evening meal when Gregory came in through the kitchen door.

She did not move immediately. It was not until she suddenly realised that the sound she could hear was her husband whistling quietly that she swung round to look at him.

And for a moment she hardly recognised him as the despondent, almost defeated man he had been.

For there was an awareness about him, an elasticity in his step, a light in his eyes which had been absent since he returned home. As if something had happened which had given him renewed hope.

"What's happened?" she asked sharply, on the heels of that thought.

He leaned against the dresser, looking

at her consideringly, without replying, and after a long moment she repeated her peremptory question.

"Why should you think anything could happen in this small place?" He moved then and went over to her, taking the spoon from her grasp and beginning to stir the gravy. "You should watch what you're doing, my dear. I'm hungry, and I'd hate scorched gravy with my meal."

She watched him silently, taken aback by this new behaviour on his part, trying to understand what it meant. Then out of a slowly mounting feeling of apprehension she said,

"Don't try to change the subject. What have you been doing, Gregory?"

He smiled down at her.

"I've been to Deepden Farm. I saw Marion Black again, and Jill."

"You've been there all day?"

"Not all day, no. But long enough to be offered a job and to — "

"You mean Marion offered you a

job? Doing what, for heaven's sake?" she interrupted.

"Helping her to run the farm."

"That's a surprise. You don't know anything about farming."

"So I told her, but she seems to think she could teach me."

"You mean you've accepted?" she asked incredulously, and was shaken suddenly by a wave of anger because he had been ready enough to work for Marion although he had turned down her own offer of a job.

Because he knew you didn't really want him, her conscience told her, but she refused to acknowledge the truth of that.

"No, though I must say I was tempted to say yes."

"That would have been ridiculous! You'd have been completely out of your depth," she said scornfully.

He looked at her frowningly.

"I never realised you had such a low opinion of me, Shelagh."

She coloured, knowing that her words

had been prompted by the very real fear that once he was established in a job there would be no hope of persuading him to go away again. And this was something she wanted more than ever now.

Since he had come home he had completely disrupted her placid life, the life which she had built up so painfully for herself and her children. And his presence made it dangerous for her to see James as often as she had done before.

Looking back, it seemed impossible that so short a time before she had been happy, her only worry that of wondering if Diane's wedding would go off well. Now she was torn again by the uncertainties and tensions which she thought had gone for ever, and knew that until Gregory went away, she would not know another peaceful moment.

"Hi, Mom, Dad." Kate's voice interrupted her thoughts as she came into the kitchen, pulling off her school hat and flinging it with her satchel of books onto the dresser. "What have you been doing today, Dad?"

"Just walking about, love. Getting to know the district."

"Walking? All day?" she said, with all the modern youngster's horror at the idea.

"Yes. I enjoyed it, too, strange as that seems to be to you I called at Deepden Farm."

"Did you see Marion? And Jill? Is she all right? Marion'd be upset if anything happened to her. Do you like her, Dad?" Kate asked eagerly.

He laughed.

"Who? Marion or the dog?"

"Marion, of course." Shelagh banged the oven door shut and turned round, unable to resist answering that question. "He's as fascinated by her as apparently you are."

He raised his eyebrows.

"Not fascinated, Shelagh. Just taking pleasure in meeting a very fine person. And after prison it's a joy to look on beauty of any kind. Especially under the circumstances," he added deliberately.

She felt the colour surge into her face and turned back to the stove, wishing she had not spoken, and hoping that he had not noticed her reaction to his reproof.

She was grateful when Kate said innocently,

"Mom's right. I do think Marion's the greatest. I'm glad you like her, too, Dad."

"I do. She offered me a job, Kate. As farm manager."

"Oh, great! You'll like working for her, and she'll be lucky to get somebody like you."

Gregory smiled, touched and comforted by his young daughter's unfaltering trust in him.

"I turned it down, love. I wouldn't even know where to begin."

"Of course you wouldn't," Shelagh cut in. "You'd far better come into the shop."

He shook his head.

"I don't want an indoor job. In fact, I don't want a job at all. Not yet. I'm enjoying my freedom too much."

"You'll soon get tired of hanging about, Dad. You've always been so busy. And Marion could really do with help." Kate said positively.

"I don't think I'd be much help, Kate," he said ruefully. "Much as I'd like to be."

"You most certainly would not!" Shelagh cut in, momentarily forgetting the trait which Gregory shared with his elder daughter. "You'd be wasting Marion's time as well as your own."

"No, he wouldn't!" Kate cried. "He's very clever! He could do anything he wanted to, couldn't you, Dad?"

"I don't know about that, love. I think you're just a little bit prejudiced," he said, touched by her faith in him.

"I'm not. Why don't you try it?" she added coaxingly. "Marion's a super person to be with."

"That I can believe without any difficulty." He smiled, as if he was looking back on something he found both pleasant and rewarding. "All right," he said suddenly, looking directly at Shelagh. "You've convinced me, Kate. I will take the job. If only to prove that I can do it."

Shelagh stared back at him, hearing Kate's enthusiastic response as if from a long way off, slowly realising what she had done.

Knowing him so well, how could she have forgotten that both he and Diane always reacted to adverse criticism as if to a challenge? Now, through her own stupidity, she had pushed him into accepting Marion's offer, though it was the very last thing she wanted him to do.

She dished up the supper automatically, putting the food on the trolley and following Gregory to the dining room as he wheeled it along.

All through the meal she listened to her daughter and her husband making plans for the future, discussing the work he would have to do, and knew that every moment was making it more difficult for her to insist that Gregory must go away.

And seeing the evident satisfaction of the girl, the obvious trust and love she felt for the man, her undisguised delight in his return, she felt lonely and unwanted, and knew a deep stab of pain and jealousy.

Because she, who had tried and striven so hard to keep her family together, to make sure that they did not suffer more than they needed to, was the one who was now ignored and forgotten.

She got up quickly, brusquely refusing their offer of help, and after she had washed up and cleared everything away, she went up to her room to write to Diane — a letter which she knew she should have sent yesterday, but which she had not had the courage to write.

It was long past midnight when she finished the letter after several abortive attempts, thrusting it into the envelope and sealing it up before she had time to change her mind and begin it all over again. But she was still not satisfied with it when she left home next morning to go to the shop and if she had had time, would have torn it up and written another.

She was weary and unrested after an almost sleepless night, during which she had had time to go over all that had happened and to anticipate what might come. For she was not looking forward to that day.

Even yesterday she had seen sly looks at her from both her staff and the customers at the shop, and although she had waited and hoped that James would come, he had not done so by the time she locked the shop door behind her.

But even though she was expecting trouble, it was still a shock when, as she went into the village post office to send off her letter to Diane by air mail, she heard the animated talk die away, to be succeeded by a deep silence. None of the women in the shop replied to her quiet 'Good morning' and she was aware of the blood draining from her face at their attitude which proclaimed only too clearly that they had been discussing her and Gregory.

She hesitated, wanting to turn and run out of the shop, back to her home, away from these people whom she knew so well but who had suddenly become so unfriendly.

Then her innate courage came to her rescue and she lifted her chin proudly, deciding without conscious thought to carry off this situation with a high hand, as though nothing was amiss. Not to let them see by word or look that she was not glad to have Gregory home again.

"An air mail stamp, please," she said distinctly. "Diane and Neil will have arrived at their hotel now, and I want this letter to get there as quickly as possible."

"I suppose so. They'll be surprised to hear about your husband. He wasn't expected yet, was he?" the postmistress said, and Shelagh felt the tension in the atmosphere increase as the other women waited breathlessly for her answer.

"No, but we're very happy to have him back," Shelagh said, and walked out of the shop, her head held high.

She had still not recovered from that encounter when she heard a voice calling her name, and turned reluctantly as Neil's mother panted up to her.

"I was on my way to the shop to see you, Mrs. Muir," she said. "About this rumour that's going about — "

"It isn't a rumour," Shelagh interrupted quickly.

"You mean it's true? Your husband's been in prison all this time? He didn't desert you?"

"Yes."

Mrs. Carter looked at her, taken aback by her quiet admission.

"Well," she said at last. "Of course I don't blame you for not telling people the truth. What I can't understand

108

is why you've let him come back at all."

"Why shouldn't I? I'm his wife, Mrs. Carter. Would you turn your back on your husband?"

She looked uncomfortable.

"It depends on what he'd done."

Shelagh shook her head.

"It doesn't, and you know it."

"I suppose I do," Neil's mother said reluctantly. "Well, my dear, I respect you for your loyalty, though I think you might have told Rob and me the real truth. You might have trusted us, and there was Neil — "

"I'm sorry. It was so difficult. You see, Diane didn't want anybody to know, especially Neil. I've written to them today, breaking it to them — If you're writing, Mrs. Carter, will you be careful what you say? Di isn't — " She broke off, seeing the sudden guilty look in the other woman's eyes, and knew her caution had been given too late. "You've already written, haven't you?"

109

"Yesterday, and posted it. I'm sorry, Mrs. Muir."

"It can't be helped. It's my own fault, really. I shouldn't have waited — "

"I'm sorry," Mrs. Carter said again. "I didn't think — "

"Don't worry. They had to know some time and I don't suppose there's any harm done."

But as she walked on towards the shop she was not so sure. Diane had always been so bitter against her father, and it was partly her bitterness which had made Brian turn against him, too, of that Shelagh was sure. There was no knowing what she might do, how she might react to the news that Gregory was home again, especially when she heard it first through Mrs. Carter, who had probably mentioned it reproachfully, with much melodrama.

When she reached the shop she went through it to her office, already feeling worn out with the effort of putting on a brave face before the world and wondering how she was going to get through the rest of that day.

She looked up defensively when the door opened, then relaxed when she saw Dorothy come in, her kind eyes concerned.

"You're late, Mrs. Muir. I was beginning to think you weren't coming. I've brought you some coffee, if you'd like it."

"I'd love it, Dorothy. Thank you. You're always so kind to me." She hesitated, then said quickly, before she could change her mind, "I suppose you've heard — about my husband coming home?"

"Yes. Mr. Seaton told me. I — "

Shelagh looked at her in astonishment.

"James told you? When? And what did he tell you?" she asked, hardly able to believe that the one person who knew how much she dreaded everyone knowing the truth had talked about it, even to somebody as discreet as Dorothy usually was.

"Last night. He came to the shop

to see you but you'd gone. He told me — about your husband being in gaol. I'm sorry, Mrs. Muir. I hope you don't mind. He thought I ought to be told, rather than hear it from outside. He did it for the best," she finished earnestly.

"I suppose he did. Anyway, it doesn't matter. I'd have told you about it myself today."

She sighed, pushing her hair back from her forehead wearily, and Dorothy said quickly,

"You're worrying about what people are saying, aren't you? They'll soon forget, Mrs. Muir. Something else will happen and they'll start talking about that instead."

"I hope you're right, Dorothy. Thank you, my dear. You're always so kind and I do appreciate it."

Dorothy flushed with pleasure.

"I'm not the only kind one. What about all you've done for me?" She paused then said hesitantly, "Will you be coming into the shop today? If you don't want to, I can manage all right."

"Yes, of course I am." She straightened her shoulders tautly. "I've got to make the break and it might as well be now."

But it was not an easy thing to do. It hurt her to see the staff looking covertly at her, to hear conversations broken off when she came near, to know that the day's takings were disastrously down. And above all, to watch every moment for James, who before Gregory came back had called to see her at least once every day, and to watch the minutes pass without bringing him.

She waited on after she had locked up the shop, remembering that Dorothy had said he had come later the night before and found her gone, and had almost given up hope of seeing him that day when he came at last.

She went to him, holding out both her hands, feeling a surge of affection as his arms went round her, even

113

though his kiss held none of the warmth and passion of a man in love. At that moment she was too deeply glad to see him for that thought to penetrate, though before the night was out she was to remember it many times.

He held her away from him looking down at her, his eyes unsmiling.

"Well, Shelagh, how are things going? Is Gregory behaving himself?"

She frowned up at him, then as his meaning penetrated, she coloured deeply.

"Yes, he's all right, James. He's got a job helping Marion Black on her farm."

"That woman! You shouldn't have allowed him to go there. There's enough gossip without adding to it — "

"I couldn't stop him, James. I've no right now, you must see that."

He moved away from her impatiently.

"You should have sent him away at once."

"I couldn't do that either. Please,

dear, don't go on at me! I can't bear it — not after today."

He came back to her then and put his arm around her.

"Has it been very bad? What's happened?"

"Nothing I didn't expect." She leaned against him gratefully, glad that his momentary annoyance had gone. "But I think I'm being boycotted. We hardly did any business today and usually we're very busy."

"There's no end to the trouble you'll have caused yourself and me by not being firm, Shelagh," he said irritably.

"I suppose so, though they'd have had something to talk about, wouldn't they, if I had refused to have him back."

She saw a flicker of anger in his eyes and was sorry she had been so blunt, because she knew that most of his reaction was fear that now Gregory had come back, she would not want him, James, any more.

She knew she ought to say something

to reassure him, but somehow, although she could understand how he was feeling, she could not bring herself to do so.

"You're probably right," he said at last, heavily. "Are you ready to go home, my dear? I'll take you, if you are."

"No, not yet. I've still got some paper work to do."

"I'll wait for you," he offered.

"No, don't, please. I'd rather you didn't. You see — "

"I see one thing. You can't be bothered with me now. Isn't that it?" he said, a dull red flush staining his forehead.

"You know that isn't true! Don't you see, darling, we can't go on as if Gregory isn't here? Things can't be the same."

"Why not? You said he didn't mean anything to you."

"I know I did and it's true, but I've got to think of the children. I can't precipitate a scandal."

"No, because there's one already."

"Well, a bigger scandal," she said wearily. "Dorothy says people will find something else to gossip about soon, and she's probably right. Be patient for a few days, James. Things will be easier then."

"I'll have to be, if you say so."

"Thank you, my dear. I'll see you tomorrow?"

"I don't know," he said stiffly. "Perhaps. Goodnight, Shelagh."

She followed him to the door and watched him go through the shop and let himself out with his key, before going back into her office again, feeling even more dispirited and exhausted.

The last thing she wanted to do was to quarrel with James, who had been so good to her over the past months, yet she knew she had had to say what she did.

Because now Gregory was home and the village was seething with gossip about them both, she and James would have to be doubly careful to give people no real grounds for further malice. They would be watched, she was sure, and no matter how circumspect they were, she knew that she was going to have to accept the loss of many whom she had looked upon as friends. And she didn't want James to suffer as well because of her.

She began to collect the papers on her desk together and thrust them into a drawer, too weary to do any work that night.

There was no end to the problems which Gregory's refusal to go away had brought to her, and she could only hope and pray that nothing would happen to make the situation worse than it already was.

Whatever the outcome, she was sure of one thing. That she was the one who was going to suffer the most because of what Gregory had done all those months ago. Perhaps he might have paid the penalty, but to her, as she walked wearily home, it seemed as if having done so, he was now in a fair way to finding happiness and peace of mind.

Whereas for her the clouds were quickly darkening and she could see nothing in the future for her but frustration and trouble.

6

IT was a warm and sunny day and as he walked briskly towards the farmhouse, Gregory whistled happily, feeling relaxed and peaceful now he had made his decision, even though it was one which he had felt compelled to make because of Shelagh's lack of confidence in him.

He knocked at the kitchen door when he arrived and after a moment's hesitation, pushed it open. There was no one there and he stood for a minute wondering what he ought to do.

Then he heard a horse whinny and Marion's voice answering, and went towards the stables on the other side of the yard.

Marion came out as he neared them, screwing up her eyes against the sunshine, then her face lit up with a smile.

"It's you, Gregory. Have you — you haven't come to tell me you've changed your mind?"

"Yes. Am I too late?"

"Of course not. Come into the house and we'll talk about it."

"Where's Jill this morning?" he asked, falling into step beside her.

"Sam's taken her with him onto the moors."

"Then she's better?"

"Almost, but never mind her for the moment. Tell me why you've changed your mind."

He hesitated, knowing he could not tell her the real reason, which was that his wife had so little faith in him that, in the depth of his hurt, he had snatched at the chance to show her, if he could, how wrong she was.

And, he admitted honestly to himself, to demonstrate perhaps that she had been equally wrong when she had refused to make the fresh start he had pleaded for. That was something he could not tell to anyone. It was private, between himself and Shelagh only.

"I think I know the reason," Marion said, when he did not answer, and his eyes took on a wary look which disappeared when she added, "I've been talking to Kate, you see."

He laughed.

"Then you're under no illusions."

"None at all. She says you're so clever, you can do anything you want to."

"She's prejudiced, I'm afraid, but you can be sure of one thing. I'll try to make her faith in me come true in this job, Marion."

Her eyes smiled into his.

"I know you will. When can you start?"

"Now, if you like, but I want to tell you something about myself before you commit yourself."

She made a negative movement with her hands.

"I don't want to hear it. I'm backing my instinct."

He took her hands in his, almost

overwhelmed by her trust in him, especially as so few people seemed to share that trust.

"I appreciate that, Marion, but I still want to tell you. I owe you that much. And if you change your mind, as others have done, I'll understand."

She pulled her hands away from his and went to sit on the settle under the window.

"All right. Tell me if you want to, though it won't make any difference. Come and sit here."

She patted the cushion beside her, but he shook his head.

"No. I'm better if I'm on the move. Marion, have you heard anything about what happened?"

"Only from Kate and she didn't have it clear. Apart from one thing. She was sure her father hadn't done anything wrong."

He smiled then, but only for a moment.

"That's my Kate. I wish I was as certain."

She frowned.

"What do you mean by that?"

"I don't remember what happened at all, Marion. I couldn't believe it when the police came early that morning and found my car damaged and reeking of whisky."

"But it really was?"

"Yes. No doubt about it." He pushed back his dark hair with its silver streak from his forehead. "And I was the only person who'd been driving it."

"You're sure about that?"

"Yes. I'd come in very late that night. I'd been to a confinement. I can remember that all right. It was a first baby and the birth was a difficult one. I was worried about it because the mother was nearly forty. I'd wanted her to go into hospital but she wouldn't leave her husband and she said she had faith in me."

He stopped, his mouth taut with painful memories as he looked back to the last time when anyone had had such complete faith in him as a doctor and as a man.

"And then?" Marion prompted quietly.

"The baby was born at last, a fine little son, and she was all right, too, though tired. I had a drink with the father before starting for home. Only one, but he insisted on giving me the rest of the bottle to take back with me. I started off I can remember that quite clearly, but afterwards nothing. A complete blank."

"There was an accident?"

"Yes. They said I'd been on the wrong side of the road coming round a sharp bend and I'd crashed into another car, injuring the driver and her son, then driven off. The boy died," he finished heavily, "but he wouldn't have done if he'd had immediate attention. Attention I could have given to him."

"Nobody saw the accident?"

"No. There was only the evidence of the woman in the car."

"And they took her word?"

"Why shouldn't they? I don't blame them for that. I wasn't the ideal witness for myself, though that wasn't surprising because it was discovered later, when I became ill in prison, that I'd been suffering from a depressed skull fracture." He touched the silver streak in his hair. "It caused this."

"Then the child's death wasn't really your fault," she said eagerly. "You ought to apply to be put back on the Register again."

He paced the length of the kitchen before answering.

"It's not as easy as that. I wish I could make you understand, Marion."

"You can try," she said quietly.

He was silent for a while, his eyes blank, withdrawn into his own bitter thoughts. Then he said at last, bleakly,

"You see, it could so easily be true. Oh, I know concussion and a depressed fracture can make you do things you wouldn't do normally, but so can a consciousness of guilt. You can forget because you don't want to remember."

"Perhaps you can, but there's still a reasonable doubt. And even if there wasn't, you've got so much to give, Gregory. Can't you see that?"

He shook his head.

"I couldn't do my job without knowing the truth. I'd — I'd always be wondering, unsure of myself. I don't suppose you can understand that, can you?"

"Yes, easily, even though I think you're quite wrong and one day you'll find that out." She got up abruptly. "Until then I'll be very glad to have you working here with me."

"Thank you," he said gratefully, then looked at her keenly, his doctor's diagnostic brain sensing something behind her words which he did not understand. "As long as you're sure it isn't going to hurt you having me here."

She made an impatient movement.

"How can I be sure of that? At least, if I'm capable of being hurt, I'm living, aren't I?" she asked challengingly.

"Anyway, I've told you. I don't care what other people think or say about me. When will you start?"

"Now, if you'll have me."

"Good. You do understand you'll have to be here by six o'clock each morning? Is that too early for you?"

He smiled, feeling a lightening of the shadow which had oppressed him while he had talked about the past. The shadow which lay like a black curtain between one part of his life and the other and which prevented him from remembering the real truth of what had happened that fateful night.

"I'm used to early rising. Shelagh can't get accustomed to coming down in the morning and finding me already in the kitchen, with breakfast over and done with. She'll be glad to have me out of the house all day."

He did not notice the flash of anger in Marion's eyes at his rueful words, and when she spoke she did not betray her feelings in her voice.

"Perhaps she will, but you'd better

ring her, hadn't you, to let her know where you are?"

"No. She knows I've come to see you about the job. She won't worry if I'm away all day, or even know," he added. "She's at the shop most of the time."

"So she is," Marion agreed drily. "Come along then, and I'll introduce you to Barney and Len." She looked at him measuringly. "I'll have to find you some overalls to wear. I think John's — my husband's, would fit you. Would you mind wearing his, for today anyway?"

"I'll be proud to," he said quietly, and she looked at him without answering before leading the way out of the house towards the outbuildings.

He followed her, puzzled by her expression, but he had very little time after that to think about anything except the work which was given to him to do and which he did so slowly with his unskilled hands.

It was a surprise when Kate came

into the barn where he was working and thrust her arm companionably through his.

"Hi, Dad. Marion said I'd find you here. How's it going?"

"All right, I think, though I'm not sure if the men or Marion would agree," he laughed. "Anyway, what are you doing here? Why aren't you at school?"

"Because it's nearly half past four, and I've come for my ride. Didn't Marion tell you I always come on two afternoons and Saturday morning?"

"No, she probably thought I'd know. Where are your riding togs? You're not going out in those clothes, surely?"

"Of course not! I keep them here. I'll go and change now and — " She broke off as Marion came into the barn. "I found him all right. He was in here."

Marion smiled.

"Good. I came to see if you'd like to ride with us, Gregory."

"Oh, yes, Dad, that'd be great!" Kate said enthusiastically.

"It's years since I've been on horse-back, and I've nothing to wear," he protested.

"I was wondering — I've looked out John's breeches and jacket. I think they'll fit you pretty well, though I'm not sure about boots. John took size nine — "

"So do I. It sounds attractive, Marion. I'd like to come. Can I try them on?"

"Of course. Come along and see if they'll fit."

When he came out of the bedroom into which she had taken him, walking rather gingerly in John's boots which were wearable though not exactly comfortable, he found Marion and Kate waiting for him.

"You look great, Dad," Kate said at once.

"I always think riding clothes suit most men," Marion said quietly.

"And women!" Gregory finished. "I'm lucky to be going out with you two. You both look wonderful."

But although he included Kate in his compliment, he knew that it was really Marion he meant. In jodhpurs and a silk shirt, the collar open to show the strong column of her throat, she looked magnificent.

Strange, he thought, as they went out into the yard where the three horses were waiting. Taken feature by feature, there was no beauty there, as she had said, yet the whole woman had a strength and fineness which he found fascinating and, as he admitted to himself, rather dangerous.

Though he had no time to dwell upon that thought then. He needed all his faculties just to stay on the horse for the first few minutes, and after that to remember everything he had known when he last rode many years before.

They did not go very far that day, only as far as the first moor. Then Marion wheeled her horse and said,

"We'll go back now, I think."

"Oh, why. We've hardly come out," Kate said.

"Maybe, but your father's had enough for one day. Oh, yes you have," she added as Gregory protested. "You may not think it now, but you wait until tomorrow. Come on, Kate. I'll race you to the big elm."

Gregory watched them set out before following at a more decorous pace, reaching them in time to congratulate Kate on winning.

When they rode into the yard again, he slid from his horse, patting its neck gratefully, before helping Marion and Kate down.

"I enjoyed that. Thank you, Marion," he said quietly, as they turned to go into the house.

"I'm glad. We must do it again, next time Kate comes," she said. "See you after you've changed. You'd better have a hot bath. I've left towels etc. in your room."

When he came downstairs at last, Kate and Marion were already in the kitchen.

"I waited for you, Dad. We may as

well go home together," Kate said, as soon as he came in.

"But it isn't time yet. I've a couple of hours work still to do — "

"Leave it for today, Gregory," Marion said. "You've worked hard. You'll probably be very tired tonight."

He frowned worriedly.

"But I don't want special treatment."

She laughed.

"You won't get it, either, after today, believe me. Now get off home, both of you." She hesitated, then added questioningly, "Would you like to use the jeep to get back and forth each day?"

"That'd be wonderful, but won't it be depriving you?"

"No. We're very well off. We've got two — the old one which I'm offering you and which will probably break down again and again, and the one I use. So you see, I don't really deserve any thanks."

He smiled down at her, taking her hand in both of his.

"I know you by now, Marion, I think, so I'll just say thank you very much, for everything you've done for me today."

She looked at him, a smile curving her lips.

"It's a pleasure, Gregory," was all she said, and as they went out into the yard, he knew he would not have wanted her, at that point, to say anything else.

He was very silent as he drove home, and was glad that Kate's chatter did not appear to need an answer.

Shelagh got up when they came into the living room and said sharply,

"At last! You're very late, Kate. Where have you both been till now?"

"At the farm. Dad came riding with us and Marion had to find him togs, and that delayed us. It was super."

Shelagh looked at Gregory.

"You've been at the farm? All day?" she asked.

"Yes, of course."

"Working?"

"Yes," he said again and smiled, a

smile which made her look at him suspiciously. "And am I tired now! Marion warned me I would be and she was right. But even so, as Kate says, it was super! I've thoroughly enjoyed it."

"I'm glad to hear it." Shelagh felt the words catch in her throat as she remembered her own worrying day. "It's more than I've done."

"Why? What's gone wrong?"

"You ask that? Don't you realise everybody knows now you've been in prison? It's been awful today, in the village, at the shop. Everything's gone wrong."

She felt the tears rise in her throat and choked them back, determined not to give way in front of him, even while she wanted to hurt him as she had been hurt that day.

"They'll forget about it soon enough — "

"Perhaps they will, but while they're doing that, I'll be ruined! We hardly sold a thing at the shop today."

"I'm sorry, Shelagh, but there's nothing I can do about it. It's something which has to be faced and overcome. I warned Marion about it, too, but she didn't seem to mind." His expression softened and he smiled. "She's a grand fighter, that girl. She must have learned her courage in a hard school."

"She isn't the only one who's had to do that! We've all had to — me, Brian, Diane — but you don't care!"

"Of course I care," he said impatiently, "but I can't see it's done either Diane or Brian any harm. I've warned you before, Shelagh. Don't try to shelter them from life. You can't do it and if you try, they'll turn against you in the end. Be careful you're not left entirely alone, then. Don't alienate everybody who loves you," he finished more gently.

He turned away as he spoke and she watched him go out of the room, realising suddenly that the droop had gone from his shoulders. His back was straight and proud again and she was vaguely aware of an odd feeling, almost of regret, which was gone almost as soon as it had come. A regret that it was not she who had given him back his self-confidence and self-respect, but a woman whom he had only recently met.

Then the remembrance of Gregory's parting words blotted out every other thought. And though she strove to repudiate them as untrue, they served to increase the uncertainty of the future which was obscured by so much doubt and confusion.

7

THE next few days passed quietly and almost placidly. Shelagh hardly saw Gregory and when she did, they treated each other like polite strangers. But in spite of that, she began to feel more hopeful about the future.

Because if they could continue to live in the same house in some sort of harmony, long enough to prepare Kate for the inevitable parting, then she would not feel she had been entirely wrong in allowing Gregory to stay for a while.

She even began to feel more hopeful about Diane. She had received cards and a letter, saying how wonderful marriage was and making no mention of her father's return, which had lulled her into a kind of security. Until the morning the second letter came.

She ran downstairs and picked it up off the floor, looking forward to hearing another instalment of her daughter's wonderful honeymoon, then stood staring at it in dismay. Because this time it was addressed not to her but to Gregory.

"Mr. G. Muir," Di had written in her largest characters and, Shelagh thought ruefully, there could be no mistaking the meaning behind that clearly written title.

Almost she was tempted to open it, then as Kate came running down the stairs, her school hat clinging precariously to the back of her head, her scarf flung round her neck, the moment was gone.

"Must you be so untidy, Kate?" she said automatically.

"Untidy? I'm not. Who's the letter from?"

"Di."

"Another one? She's getting good since she got married. What's she got to say now? Still going on about how wonderful it is to be married to Neil?"

"I don't know. This one's addressed to your father."

"To Dad? Surprise, surprise! Shall I go round by the farm and give it to him?"

"Of course not. It can wait till he comes home. I shouldn't think it's as important as all that," Shelagh said, though by the time Gregory came, much later than usual, she had begun to wish she had given in to that first impulse and ripped the envelope open.

"You're very late," she said, the tension which had been growing within her betraying itself in the sharpness of her greeting. "Where've you been?"

He looked at her in surprise.

"At the farm. Where else?"

"Till this hour? Doing what?"

"Well, if it really interests you, which I doubt," he said forthrightly, "I've been assisting at an accouchement. A bit different from anything I've been used to, but very fascinating just the same."

She moved impatiently.

"I don't know what you're talking about."

"I'd have thought it was clear enough. One of the cows was calving and as it was the cowman's day off, I stayed to help Marion." He smiled, his voice changing all the impatience leaving it. "She really is the most amazing person. She can do anything at all around that farm, and all with the minimum of fuss and trouble."

"So she should be able to. She's been farming practically all her life. You might have let me know you'd be so late."

"I'm sorry about that. It never occurred to me. You see, I didn't expect you to be worried about me."

She flushed at his words and lifted her chin defensively, realising now that the peaceful interlude they had enjoyed had disappeared again and, as she admitted, through her fault.

"Why should I be?"

"Exactly, when you don't care," he

said deliberately.

She bit back the words she wanted to say, words which would only have increased the bitterness which had lain between them from the moment she had set out the terms on which he could remain with them all. Abruptly, she held out the letter to him.

"This came for you. It's from Diane."

He took it without comment and ripped it open, reading it without any change in his expression, then crushing it between his fingers.

"Well, aren't you going to tell me what she says?" Shelagh asked when the silence became unendurable.

He shrugged.

"Read it yourself if you're interested. She only tells me to get out before she and Neil come home. To get out and stay out."

She took it from him and smoothed it out, feeling ashamed of Diane when she read the few searing lines she had written to her father.

"What are you going to do?" she asked at last.

He looked at her in surprise.

"Why, nothing! What else should I do? It's no surprise, is it? I knew we both knew how she felt and this letter only underlines it. And after all, she isn't really to blame, is she? She's taken her tone from you, Shelagh."

He stood for a moment as if waiting for her to deny it, but she could say nothing at all. Then he turned and strode out of the room.

She moved then, screwing up the letter and flinging it into the fire, feeling anger run through her like a flame. He was so unfair. He was blaming her for everything that had happened because she had been honest enough to tell him of her own change of heart.

If only he had gone away as she had asked him to. Then they would have both been spared the pain of seeing something which had once been precious to them broken and valueless.

★ ★ ★

Though when the police sergeant called a couple of days later, she was deeply glad that Gregory was there to help her.

It was he who opened the door and said in surprise,

"Sergeant Cross! What's gone wrong? Have I forgotten to do something?"

"It isn't you this time, sir. It's your son."

"Brian!" Shelagh hurried out of the living room, her eyes anxious. "What's happened to him? What's he been doing now?"

She was aware of Gregory's look of surprise and knew she ought to have told him about the trouble she had had with Brian over the past months. But she had not wanted to betray him to his father, especially as lately he seemed to have settled down at last.

"Nothing very bad, Mrs. Muir," the sergeant said soothingly. "He got mixed up in a fight outside a football ground this afternoon, that's all."

"Is he hurt?"

"Yes, though not badly. He's got a cut head and they're keeping him in hospital for a day or two in case of delayed shock and concussion. I thought I'd come along and tell you before you heard about it from some other source and got worried."

"Thank you, that was kind of you," Shelagh said.

"It is indeed. Which hospital is he in?" Gregory asked.

The sergeant told them, and as the door closed behind him Shelagh said anxiously,

"Do you think he was telling the truth, Gregory? Why should he come if Brian's only slightly hurt? He must be worse than he says."

"That doesn't follow. Anyway, we can easily make sure. Would you like to go and see him?"

"Oh, yes, I would, but it's a terrible journey, especially on a Sunday."

"Not if I borrow Marion's car. She

said I could have it any time I wanted it. I'll ring her now and see if it will be all right."

"No, don't — " she began, then stopped because he was already out of the room; and by the time he came back she had managed to overcome in some measure the distaste she felt at accepting any favours from Marion Black.

"That's all fixed up," he said. "I'm to go and get the car now, so that we can set out first thing in the morning." He looked at her keenly, seeing the lines of worry on her forehead, and after a momentary hesitation, went to her and put a comforting arm around her shoulders. "Don't worry about him, Shelagh. He'll he all right."

She closed her eyes, feeling an intense desire to relax against him, to be held in his arms as she used to be, while he caressed all her fears away.

Then as her pulses leaped under his touch she shivered suddenly, uncontrollably, and at that instinctive movement he let her go at once.

"Sorry," he said briefly. "I forgot. It won't happen again," and went quickly out of the room.

She did not move for a while after he had gone, feeling physically incapable of doing so; glad that he had misunderstood that sudden flare of awareness within her, that unexpected betrayal by her body which had taken her by surprise and made her afraid of her own desires and weakness.

He did not come back until long after she had gone to bed. She was still wide awake when she heard him come quietly up the stairs and knew a queer pang of dismay because he and Marion were so obviously on such very good terms with each other.

She turned over restlessly, telling herself that it did not matter to her how friendly they were. Yet when morning came she was still aware of an antipathy to the thought that her husband and this other woman should have apparently reached so quickly and easily such a good understanding.

Perhaps it was this feeling which made her unwilling to talk very much on the journey to the hospital where Brian had been taken. That and the fact that Gregory, too, had very little to say for himself.

It was a relief when they parked the car outside the building and found their way to the ward where he was lying.

He looked up defensively when they walked towards him, his face young and vulnerable beneath the white head bandage.

"Who told you I was here? What did you come for?" he asked ungraciously.

"Because your mother was worried," Gregory said sharply.

He hunched his shoulders.

"I didn't want her to know about it. I'm all right."

"But what happened, Brian?" Shelagh asked anxiously, seeing the familiar stubborn look harden Brian's mouth. "What were you doing?"

"I wasn't doing anything. Just walking

past with — just walking past the football ground as the crowds were coming out, and some gang started a fight."

"Why didn't you give them a wide berth then?" Gregory asked.

"Because oh, well, anyway I couldn't and the next thing one of them hit me with a bottle or something."

"Did you see who it was?"

"Mum, in that crowd? Don't be futile!"

"Sorry, Brian." Shelagh coloured at his tone. "What are the police doing about it?"

"Nothing! They don't believe a word I say. And there's supposed to be justice in this country! That's a laugh!"

"It's easy to get into trouble without meaning to, isn't it?" Gregory said quietly. "To be wrongfully accused and not to be able to prove anything to the contrary."

Shelagh looked at him in sudden awareness and was glad when Brian said sullenly,

"I knew you wouldn't believe me."

"But I do, dear," she began, "I" then stopped as she saw Gregory's lips tighten and understood what he was thinking.

That she was ready enough to accept her son's word that he was not in the wrong, but not her husband's.

"Would you like us to go to the police and try to sort things out," Gregory said at last, into the silence which had fallen.

"No, thanks. I don't want anyone to fight my battles. If they won't believe me, then I —— "

He broke off, his face changing as he looked past them down the length of the ward, all the sullenness gone from his expression in a moment.

Shelagh turned and saw a girl walking towards them, her red hair bouncing against her shoulders, straight and shining, her long legs clad in faded jeans and topped by a thick sweater.

"Hi, there," she said as she reached them. "How are you today, Bri?"

"Okay."

Brian spoke offhandedly but there was no disguising the feeling there was between him and this tall girl, as modern and 'with-it' as she could be and Shelagh had no time to adjust to this new suspicion, to hide the dismay she felt.

As Gregory got to his feet, smiling at the girl, Brian said,

"The parents, Liz. This is Liz Allan, one of the girls in my College."

"Hello," Liz said with a friendly smile. "Glad to know you. I was beginning to think Brian had been spawned or something, he said so little about his family."

Gregory grinned.

"No. Begat in the usual way."

She laughed then, gay and uninhibited.

"Good. And here he is, quite the little hero, aren't you?" she said, her words mocking but her eyes and mouth young and tender. "Saving the girl friend from a fate worse than death!"

"That's enough from you, nit," Brian

said. "Where've you been till now? You're hours late."

"To the police station. I told them what happened and everything's going to be okay."

Shelagh looked at Brian, expecting to see the sullen look come back into his face, to hear his voice hot with annoyance, but instead he only grinned and put his hand over hers.

"Trust you, Liz, to go your own way. I might have known. Thanks a lot," he added carelessly.

"Think nothing of it," she said, but Shelagh saw her hand tighten on his as she smiled down at him.

Gregory got up.

"We'll have to go, Brian, if we're going to get back home at a reasonable hour. Nice to have met you, Liz. You must get Brian to bring you home with him one weekend, so that we can show you that we're a fairly normal family after all."

"I'll do that," she promised, but Shelagh was aware that she and Brian hardly noticed they had gone, they were so engrossed in each other.

It was this disquieting truth that filled her mind to the exclusion of everything as she and Gregory drove home, so that she did not notice how strained his face was, nor the weary way he rubbed his hands over his eyes before starting the car.

She could only see this red-haired girl, the kind of girl she disliked so much, the very last one whom she wanted her son to have anything at all to do with.

"Nice girl that." Gregory's voice broke in on her troubled thoughts.

"Nice! She looks — oh, as bad as she can be."

"Rubbish, Shelagh. She's just a mod type. I liked her and I don't think there's any doubt what Brian feels!"

"That's the trouble. Do you think I want to see him caught by somebody like her? Getting married before even he has his degree, perhaps? You must have been mad to ask her to come and visit us, Gregory. We don't want her type for him!"

"Oh, don't he so hidebound!" he said impatiently. "I've told you before, you can't tie the present day youngster to your apron strings. Surely even you can see that if Liz isn't the right type for Brian, he'll find that out quicker by seeing her in his own home than any other way?"

"I might have known you'd have a good reason for not supporting me, as usual. It's the easy way out for you all the time, just like all the other modern parents. But I'm not like that. I won't stand by and see my son ruin his life."

"You'll be a fool if you interfere, Shelagh," he said.

She hunched herself away from him and did not reply, and he did not continue to reason with her.

The rest of the journey passed in silence, a silence fraught once again with resentment and tension, until when they reached home he said abruptly, without switching off the car engine or getting out to see her into the house,

"I'll take the car back to the farm in case Marion wants it. I won't be long."

He drove away and Shelagh watched until he was out of sight before going into the empty house. She was coming downstairs after taking off her hat and coat when the telephone rang and she hurried to answer it, hoping it might be James.

"Hello! Shelagh Muir speaking," she said, thinking how good it would be to talk over this latest trouble about Brian, sure that she would have all his understanding and sympathy.

But it was not James's voice which answered her. Instead Marion Black said briskly,

"It's Marion here. I'm ringing to tell you Gregory won't be coming home tonight."

"Why not?" Shelagh asked, taken aback by the matter of fact statement spoken in Marion's clear voice.

"Because he isn't well enough. He's had one of his splitting headaches all day. Didn't you know?"

Shelagh's fingers tightened on the receiver at the note in the other woman's voice, but before she could reply, Marion went on, "But you needn't worry about him — if you are worrying, that is. I've made up a bed in my spare room. He'll be all right. I'll take good care of him."

Shelagh heard the decisive click at the other end of the line and slowly put down the receiver, aware of a rising anger which surprised her by its intensity.

How dared Marion talk to her in such a way, as if she did not care at all that Gregory was ill. 'One of his splitting headaches', she had said, which meant that she knew he often had them.

She knew, she told herself bitterly, but he had not thought it worth his while to tell her, his wife. Instead he had apparently gone to a lot of trouble to hide that fact from her.

She sat down abruptly, most of the anger she had felt against Marion now directed towards Gregory. It was his fault that she had been put into such an invidious and difficult position. Just as everything which had happened to frustrate and distress her since he had come home could be laid at his door.

And none of it would have happened if he had had the decency to go away again as she had asked him to. Instead, aided by Marion Black, he had stayed on and now there seemed to be no hope of his ever going.

There would be no end to the trouble and unhappiness which stretched before her, and at that thought she covered her face with her hands and for the first time wept, for herself, for James, and for the ending of all the hopes she had had for the future.

8

BY the time morning came, Shelagh had recovered from that mood of despair and had made up her mind what she ought to do. Somehow she had to find out what the real position was between Marion and Gregory, whether it was only that of employer and servant, or whether there was some deeper feeling there.

When he came home that night, she told herself, she would ask him outright about it and then make her own decision in the light of what he said.

But she was not given that respite of a day in which to make up her mind how she was going to approach that subject. Instead Gregory took her by surprise, coming into the kitchen as she was clearing up after seeing Kate off to school and before she left herself for the shop.

"You're early," she said sharply. "Why have you come home now?"

"To change. I can't work in this suit. It's the only decent one I've got."

"You've had breakfast?"

"Yes, thanks," he said briefly and went out of the room.

When he came back again she had had time to remember that yesterday he had been ill, and asked quietly,

"How are you, Gregory? Are you better?"

"Yes, thanks," he said again.

"Why didn't you tell me you had bad headaches?"

He shrugged.

"There's no point in talking about them. They're something I've got to learn to live with — since this happened," and he smoothed the streak of silver across his head.

"But you told Marion!"

He frowned.

"I didn't. She recognised the signs because John, her husband, suffered in the same way. That's how she knows exactly what to do." He smiled, a warm remembering light in his eyes. "She has some magic in her fingers. She can massage the pain away so quickly. What a wonderful person she is!"

"Be careful your admiration doesn't take you by surprise one day," Shelagh said, before she could stop herself.

He looked at her without speaking for a moment, then said with emphasis,

"You've no need to worry about us, Shelagh. I know what village communities are like. I'll take good care that Marion's reputation doesn't suffer because of her kindness to me. Not that she cares what anybody thinks or says about her, but I do — for her."

He turned away on the words and left the house, and she stood for a long while, hearing his words echoing in her ears.

She knew now the answer to her question, knew the degree of feeling which existed, on Gregory's side without doubt and, she suspected, on Marion's also.

But instead of that knowledge bringing her the relief she might have expected, it only seemed to deepen the depression and frustration which had been with her from the moment he had come home.

* * *

While she was at the shop she had too much to do to think about Gregory's answer, but by the time she reached home that evening, it was again in the forefront of her mind.

So that when Kate came hurrying in a few minutes later, saying,

"Tea ready, Mom? I've got a meeting at school tonight and I haven't much time. When does Di arrive tomorrow?" she realised with a sense of shock that for the past few days she had hardly given a thought to her elder daughter.

"I don't know, Kate, but I suppose

she'll come along to see us as soon as she can manage it."

Kate looked at her with the direct gaze which was so like her father's.

" — you really think she will, Mom?"

"Of course. Why shouldn't she?"

"Well, you know what she's like when she gets a bee buzzing in her bonnet."

"Yes," Shelagh said slowly. "I do, but this time — Oh, of course she'll come, Kate, just as soon as she gets back. She'll be too anxious to tell us all about the honeymoon to keep away."

She was so sure that she was right that she came home early from the shop and spent the rest of the afternoon baking Diane's favourite cake, expecting all the time to hear her ring at the door bell. But when at last she heard those welcome chimes and hurried to answer them, she could not hide her disappointment when she saw James waiting outside and not Diane.

"It's you!" she said. "I'd hoped it — "

She stopped, realising she had upset him when she saw his dark frown.

"I'm sorry you're disappointed. If I'd known you didn't want to see me, I wouldn't have come."

"Of course I'm glad to see you, James," she said quickly. "I always am."

"Are you? I'm not sure about that. In fact, I'm beginning to wonder if recently you've been avoiding me deliberately. Have you?"

"No, I have not."

"Then why be so unwelcoming?"

"I wasn't, not really. It's just that — well, I was expecting it to be Diane, back from her honeymoon."

"I'm sorry you were disappointed, my dear," he said, at his driest.

"Oh, James, you're making a fuss about nothing — "

"Am I? Do you know how many days it is since I've seen you alone?"

"Yes, but that doesn't mean I don't

164

want you to come."

He smiled then, and went past her into the house, closing the door firmly behind him.

"I'm glad to know that, my dear." He bent and kissed her deliberately, holding her tightly against him. "I love you, Shelagh. You know that, don't you?"

"Yes, but — "

"But what?"

"Things are different now. Gregory's home and — "

He frowned.

"What difference does that make. He must know what the true position is." His arm tightened possessively. "Don't let him spoil things for us, darling. We were so happy together before he came back."

She leaned away from him, trying to loosen his grip upon her.

"We will be again, dear, but don't you see, for a little while we must go carefully. Try to understand, James."

"I do try, but I find it very difficult."

165

He smiled at her ruefully. "I'm not a saint, my darling. I'm a man and I love you, very much. I don't want to wait for you for ever."

His mouth came down passionately on hers and for a moment she was lost in the joy of knowing she was loved and wanted. Then she remembered and drew away from him, breathing quickly.

"No, love, we mustn't. Not here."

His fingers tightened painfully on her shoulders.

"What's the matter with you?" he demanded angrily. "You never used to be like this."

"I know, but don't you understand how difficult things are, James?"

He gave her a little shake.

"No, I can't. What difference can it make to us that Gregory's come home?"

"You're forgetting. He's still my husband."

"But only in name," he said fiercely.

"Yes, of course. Only — "

166

"Only what?"

She looked up at him, her eyes dark with trouble.

"I think I must have been a little mad, James. When Gregory wasn't here everything seemed so simple. But now he's back and I can see clearly — there can't be any future for us," she finished simply.

"Shelagh, sometimes I could murder you!" he said in exasperation. "Nothing has changed. You would have got a divorce before. You can still get one now."

"That's nonsense. I've no grounds for divorce."

"Of course you have."

She looked at him in astonishment.

"What grounds? What do you mean?"

He sighed irritably.

"They always say the wife is the last person to hear about what's going on, but I never believed it before. Don't you know what everyone is saying?"

"No. What can they say?"

"Plenty, believe me. For instance,

that Gregory has been known to stay all night at the farm with Marion Black. You can't blame people for believing the worst, my dear."

"I can," she said, almost fiercely. "He only stayed there once, because he was ill. Marion rang to tell me what had happened. She wouldn't have done that it there had been anything — anything like you're hinting."

He laughed without mirth.

"And you really swallowed that? For heaven's sake, my love, how naïve can you get? A child of ten wouldn't have been deceived by that corny story."

She pulled away from him in annoyance.

"It was true!" she cried. "I know it was."

"Rubbish!" He slid his hands down her arms, taking her wrists in a strong grip. "But even if you were right, don't you see, darling, that this is our chance? Our chance for you to get your freedom easily. He'll be glad to give it to you to guard Marion Black from being cited as the co-respondent."

She was silent for a while, looking at him as if she was seeing him properly for the first time.

"I couldn't do that," she said at last. "It wouldn't be fair. Anyway, isn't there something about condoning? If he continues to live here with me — "

"But he won't, if you play your cards right," he said triumphantly. "He's got somewhere to live now — in one of the empty cottages on Marion's farm."

"A cottage?"

"Yes. Surely you don't imagine that she hasn't already offered to let him have one of them?"

"Why should she? I don't understand you, James- — "

He shook his head in mock dismay.

"What a little innocent you are, Shelagh. It would be very unusual if she didn't, under the circumstances. Everything's beginning to come our way, my darling. Can't you see that?"

His mouth came down on hers, suddenly, without any warning, but this time with a difference. For a moment she relaxed against him, feeling a surge of emotion course through her, returning his kisses with a matching fervour.

Then her mood changed and she twisted her mouth away from his, knowing without any doubt that here, in this house into which Gregory might walk at any moment, she ought not to respond to the passion which was burning through him.

"No, don't. Stop it." She pushed against him with all her strength. "Let me go, James."

He took his arms away so abruptly that she staggered and almost fell. Then as she steadied herself she felt a surge of fear as she saw the naked anger in his eyes.

"So that's it? Now Gregory's back you don't want me any more. History's repeating itself with a vengeance, isn't it?" he finished bitterly.

She put out an unsteady hand to him.

"No, that isn't true. It's just — Oh! everything's confused. I don't seem to be able to think properly. You'll have to give me time, dear. That's all I need. Time to get used to the idea — "

Her voice trailed away, but she saw with relief the look of anger slowly leave his eyes.

"Very well, I will. As long as you remember this, Shelagh. I mean to claim you as my wife one day, and I don't intend to wait very long before doing so."

He bent and kissed her, but gently this time without any of the passion he had shown before.

"Yes, one day," she agreed quietly. "Thank you, my dear. You're very kind to me — kind and tolerant and I do appreciate it. I'm sorry — about everything," she finished obscurely and with difficulty.

When he had gone she sat down wearily, pushing her hair back from her hot forehead, thinking of what he had told her.

Could it be true that Gregory and Marion were lovers. That when he had stayed the night with her it had not been because he was ill but because they could not bear to be apart from one another any longer?

Yet it seemed unnecessarily complicated, especially if she really had an empty cottage to give to Gregory. It must only be malicious gossip, gossip of the kind which had circulated about Marion before she had married John Black.

She breathed a sigh of relief, feeling as if a weight had rolled off her shoulders, but it was only momentary. The next moment she had remembered what Gregory had said to her so recently.

"You've no need to worry about Marion. I'll take good care of her reputation," and all the doubts came flooding back and with them the certainty that James had been right.

Gregory's care for Marion's reputation was their opportunity to get the divorce which would leave them free to marry, but that conviction brought with it no peace of mind.

Instead she felt only a deep resentment against the woman who had so easily taken Gregory away from her, who was going to be given the love and happiness which had once been so precious to her. A resentment which extended to the man who had told her the truth of what had been going on at Deepden Farm.

Then she sat up very straight, lifting her chin proudly. telling herself that this was not so. Marion had not taken her husband from her because she had already given him up when she told him that although he had come back into her life, there was no place in it for him.

Now the only thing that remained was for her to ask Gregory to give her the evidence necessary to obtain a divorce. Then she would be free to marry James and be happy again.

She shivered suddenly, her mind

shying away from that thought, from its ultimate finality.

"It's only to be expected," she told herself, getting up and moving restlessly about the room. "After more tenty years of marriage, anyone would think it a terrific step to take."

And she deliberately shut her mind on the unbidden and unexpected aversion she suddenly felt to the idea of living for the rest of her life as James's wife.

9

SHELAGH had still not recovered from the shock of that sudden self knowledge when the door bell rang again and she went to answer it.

For a moment, because of her own inward perturbation, she did not realise who was there.

It was only when Diane said gaily, "Wake up, Mom. Don't you know who it is? Surely you haven't completely forgotten me in a fortnight?" that she was able to pull herself together and welcome her daughter as she had planned to.

"Of course not, darling." She put her arm around Diane and pulled her into the house, kissing her warmly. "It's lovely to see you. Kate and I have been longing to hear all about everything. She'll be mad that she's missed you."

"There'll be plenty of other times. Anyway, I really haven't time to stop now. I've got a couple more calls to make, then I've got to get off home to cook a meal for Neil."

"But you've enjoyed yourselves?"

"We've had the most wonderful time, Mom. It was great."

"That's good, my dear. Why didn't you bring Neil with you?"

"His father had things he wanted to show him on the farm. Anyway — " She stopped and Shelagh looked at her quickly, recognising the determination in her daughter's expression.

"What is it, Diane?" she asked quietly.

"I wanted to see you alone first because honestly, you must have been mad to let Dad stay here, Mom. Why didn't you make him go away again? When I got Mother Carter's letter, I could hardly believe it."

"Couldn't you. And Neil? Did he think I ought to have sent your father away?"

176

Diane shrugged.

"Oh, well, you know Neil. He's so easy going. That's why he's such a lamb. But it doesn't alter the facts, Mom. You shouldn't have let him stay."

Shelagh made an impatient movement.

"I had no alternative, Di. Even you must see that. He hadn't anywhere else to go and we — I'd used his money, remember, to buy this house and the shop"

"I should think so, too!" her daughter interrupted. "You'd every right to look after yourself and us. Mrs. Carter says he's started working at Deepden Farm and everyone's talking about him and Marion Black already."

"Nonsense," Shelagh said impatiently. "You ought to know your father by now. He isn't like that."

"That's what you think! All men are like that if you give them half a chance."

Shelagh smiled at her sweeping indictment.

"Even Neil?" she asked gently.

"Yes, though I'll take good care nothing like that ever happens! But you must see he's got to go away, Mom. It's so humiliating having him here, now everybody knows about him."

"There's nothing I can do about it, dear."

"Then I'll have to do something myself."

Shelagh got up quickly.

"No, Di, you're not to. This isn't your business. Please keep out of it."

"I will not! It is my business, mine and Brian's, too. How do you think he'll like it when he's got to tell his girl friend about Dad?"

Shelagh frowned at her.

"How long have you known about this girl, Di?"

Diane looked at her uncomfortably.

"Oh, a few weeks. Why?"

"And you didn't think it worth while to tell me about her?"

"Why should I? It was up to Brian. Anyway, it doesn't matter now. He's told you himself."

Shelagh shook her head.

"He didn't. We met her, your father and I, when we went to see Brian while he was in hospital."

"In hospital? What's wrong with him?"

"Nothing very much. He's quite better now. He got mixed up in a fight outside a football ground and was knocked on the head."

"Trust Brian! Always in trouble."

"This time, apparently, he was trying to protect the girl, Elizabeth, from the mob."

Diane looked at her shrewdly.

"You don't like her, do you?"

"I don't know her well enough to give an opinion," Shelagh said coldly.

"What! They can both come and stay with me. It'll be more fun for them and you can get to know Liz gradually. You'll like her, Mom. Neil and I think she's great." She got up suddenly. "Look at the time! I must fly! Neil will be coming in for his meal and there'll be nothing ready. See you, Mom. Love to Kate."

Shelagh went with her to the door, watching as she got into Neil's Land-Rover and drove off before going back into the house, feeling depressed and lonely.

The first meeting with her daughter since her marriage had fallen quite flat, she thought resignedly. She had expected her to be concerned mainly with her own affairs, to have most of her interest concentrated on her new husband.

What she had not been prepared for was to find that her main reason for wanting her father to go away was because of the effect his homecoming might have on her own relationship with her new in-laws. Which she found difficult to accept from the girl who had only been concerned with her, Shelagh's, happiness.

Well, perhaps it would have some good effect, if Neil's wiser counsels made her change her uncompromising attitude to her father.

And as the days passed and she neither saw nor heard of Diane, she began to hope that this was what had happened and to feel more relaxed and hopeful. A feeling which was helped by the fact that James and she were friends once more. Not perhaps quite on the old footing. There was still a little constraint between them, a constraint which Shelagh tried to ignore and which she hoped would gradually disappear. Because in spite of their recent clashes, she was still grateful to James for all he had done for her and was thankful that they were good friends again.

She was thinking about him when she walked to the shop a few days later, looking forward to seeing him that day, wondering what he had meant when he told her over the telephone that morning that he had something surprising for her.

Dorothy came to meet her when she let herself in, her eyes bright with anticipation.

"Can you spare a few minutes before you begin work, Mrs. Muir?" she asked eagerly. "I want to show you something."

"Of course, Dorothy. What is it? Something new and glamorous you've thought up?"

"Yes. Mr. Seaton's seen it and he likes it. I hope you will, too."

Shelagh looked at her in surprise.

"What's it got to do with him?"

"As if you didn't know!" Dorothy laughed. "Come and I'll show it to you."

She led the way upstairs to the workrooms on the top floor and Shelagh followed her, still pulled by her words.

Though she was not left long in doubt. Dorothy turned left at the top of the stairs and stopped at the first door.

"Here it is," she said, and flung open the door rather dramatically, standing back to give Shelagh precedence.

She went in slowly, then stood quite

still, her eyes widening as she saw the gown, displayed on one of the window models. It was long and elegant, fashioned of a heavy gold brocade, and glittered extravagantly in the brilliant light which was directed onto it.

"There!" Dorothy's voice sounded triumphantly from just behind her. "What do you think of it, Mrs. Muir?"

"Why, it's really lovely, Dorothy. You've surpassed yourself this time. Who's the lucky person you've designed it for?"

"Why, you of course." Dorothy's voice was surprised and puzzled. "Who else?"

"For me? But I didn't order it."

Shelagh swung round to her assistant, wondering which of them was dreaming. How could this beautiful dress be hers when this was the first she had known about it?

"Of course you didn't!" Dorothy laughed. "But Mr. Seaton did, for you to wear at the Civic Dinner next week.

Surely you haven't forgotten about it?"

"It's the first — "

Shelagh stopped, catching her breath on the surge of anger which swept through her, swallowing the stinging words she had been going to say.

Because this was not Dorothy's fault. It would not be fair to blame her when all she had done was to carry out instructions given to her by the other partner in the business.

It was James who was at fault. James, who had once again not bothered to consult her before making plans and arrangements as he had done more than once before.

"Don't you like it, Mrs. Muir? Is there something wrong with it?"

Dorothy's worried voice recalled her from her resentful thoughts and she said quickly,

"Of course not. It's really very beautiful indeed. I congratulate you, Dorothy."

"That's good." She breathed a deep sigh of relief. "You had me worried for a moment. Shall I help you to put it on? Mr. Seaton's waiting in your office to see how you look in it."

"Is he?"

She was aware again of that unreasoning surge of anger against James because once again he had taken it for granted that she would be grateful for anything he did for her. That she had no mind of her own. Well, this time, she told herself grimly, he would find he had done so once too often. "I won't put it on now, Dorothy," she said aloud. "I'll just go down and have a word with him about it."

She was aware of the other woman's puzzled gaze following her as she went downstairs, and was glad when she was at last out of sight.

She thrust open her office door and went in. James got up from his seat behind her desk, the smile dying on his lips when he saw her.

"Where's your gown? Why aren't you wearing it? Didn't Dorothy show it to you?"

"Yes, she did. She also told me that you ordered it for me to wear at a dinner you think you're taking me to next week."

He frowned at her tone.

"And what is wrong with that? You sound as if you don't like the idea."

"Is that surprising? Who do you think I am? Some little drab who hasn't a dress fit to wear to accompany you to your dinner? Who'd be grateful to be told she was going somewhere with you, without the courtesy of being asked first if she wanted to go?"

He stared at her in complete astonishment.

"What's come over you, Shelagh? This isn't the first time I've arranged to take you out without asking you first. I intended the whole thing to be a surprise for you," he added, a note of real injury in his voice.

She felt the annoyance die within her as she acknowledged the truth of what he had said, and knew she should have told him long ago that she objected to his high-handed treatment of her.

But she had never done so because she had been lonely. She had been so grateful to him for the way in which he had helped her, that she had accepted his well meant kindness without protest.

It was only now, quite suddenly, as if she had reached a new maturity, that she knew she could no longer bear to be treated like an irresponsible child without a mind of her own.

"I'm sorry, James," she said quietly, "but I can't accept your expensive present. And I can't come with you to the dinner either."

A tide of red coloured his face.

"Why not? You'd have jumped at the chance a few weeks ago."

"Perhaps I would, but I've told you before — everything's changed now Gregory's home."

She saw anger in his eyes.

"And I've asked you before — what has that got to do with it?"

"Everything. I thought you under-stood, James. But I'm not going to argue with you about it now. You'll have to take somebody else this time. What about Dorothy?"

"Dorothy! It's you I want to take. Now listen to me, Shelagh," he said, his voice rising angrily. "I'm not going to put up with — "

He broke off as the door opened and Dorothy came in, hesitating and colouring faintly at the silence which greeted her entry.

"I'm sorry to interrupt, Mrs. Muir. I didn't think you'd still be busy. I'll come back later."

"It's all right, Dorothy," James said sharply. "I'm going myself. I'll talk to you later, Shelagh, when you've had time to think about things and, perhaps, come to your senses again."

He stalked out of the room on the words and Shelagh sat down at her desk, pushing back her hair from her forehead wearily.

Dorothy watched her for a moment,

then asked anxiously,

"Do you feel all right? Can I get you anything? A drink? Some coffee?"

"I'd love some coffee, Dorothy, if it isn't too much trouble," Shelagh said gratefully.

"It's no trouble at all. I won't be a tick."

She hurried from the office and Shelagh sat back in her chair and leaned her head on her hands, feeling ashamed now of her anger.

It had been inexcusable of her to fling back James's kindness in his face in such a way, especially as she had never before allowed him to know how much this kind of thing irritated her.

But his 'surprise' this time, coming as it did on top of all the worries and heartache of the last few weeks, had been too much for her to accept gracefully.

By the time Dorothy came back with a pot of coffee for her she had made up her mind to go and see him and apologise. And at the same time she

189

intended to make it clear that under no consideration could she go to the Civic Dinner with him. That in future she could not go anywhere with him. Not while Gregory was at home.

When he went away, if he did, then perhaps they could once again take up their relationship where it had been left off when Gregory arrived home so suddenly.

But instead of that thought bringing with it a lifting of the heart, as it would have done a few weeks ago, she felt only a sense of loss which surprised her by its intensity.

10

LUCKILY for her peace of mind Shelagh was kept much too busy during the rest of that day to do more than remember her quarrel with James fleetingly.

When she at last closed and locked the shop door behind her she should have been feeling happy, because the excellent day's trading must have meant that people were already beginning to forget, had stopped boycotting her.

Instead she felt depressed and weary, wanting only to get home, take off her shoes and spend a quiet evening relaxing in the peace of her own home.

But even that was denied to her.

Diane got up eagerly as she went into the living room.

"At last, Mom," she said with relief. "I was beginning to think you'd had an accident or something. Where've you been. And where's Kate?"

"I've been at the shop and Kate's staying late at school tonight, rehearsing for the Open Day choir." She sat down in an easy chair and kicked off her shoes. "It's nice to see you, dear," she added. "We were beginning to think you'd forgotten the way here."

She saw the flush colour Diane's face and was immediately sorry for her momentary spasm of irritation, but before she could say anything, her daughter answered quickly,

"Of course I haven't, Mom. It's just that I've been so busy. I'd no idea how much work there is just keeping house and cooking for Neil and me. Anyway," she added honestly, "I don't want to meet Dad either."

"Then you've come at the wrong time," Shelagh said drily. "He's usually in by now."

"He won't be tonight," Diane began, then stopped, looking self conscious.

Shelagh frowned.

"How do you know that?" she asked

sharply, feeling a dawning fear.

"Because I've been to Deepden Farm before I came here and she, Marion Black, said he'd gone to market with Sam."

"What did you go there for?" Shelagh asked sharply. "What have you been doing? Tell me at once, please."

"Just what I said I'd do."

There was a note of bravado in her voice, but underneath it Shelagh thought she detected a deep uncertainty.

"What did you say to Marion?"

"I told her what I thought of her, encouraging my father to stay here and giving everybody cause to talk."

"Di, how dare you? Your father will be furious when he hears — "

Diane shrugged.

"I don't care if he is. He should have gone away — he should never have come here in the first place," she added resentfully. "Carrying on with Marion Black, making a laughing stock of you — "

"But I told you, Diane. There's no

193

truth in that rumour.

"There is," Diane said obstinately. "Mrs. Carter says you ought to be warned."

"Stop it!" Shelagh said urgently, knowing that whatever might be the truth of the relationship between her husband and Marion, she could not let her daughter continue to talk in such a way. "You've no right to repeat such rubbish."

"It's not rubbish. You're as bad as Neil. He says I ought to mind my own business, too. Marion Black's got you all on her side."

Diane's lips trembled and the unshed tears glittered in her eyes, and seeing them, Shelagh did not give way to the amusement her daughter's wail had brought to her, an amusement which had relieved some of the tension which had been building up within her.

"Don't be silly, Di. Neil and I are hardly likely to take Marion's side against you."

"But you are doing, and I was

only trying to do what is best for you and Neil. And now you're both against me."

The tears were beginning to flow in earnest and Shelagh spoke more sharply that she had meant to, in an effort to stem them, knowing how easily her daughter could give way to her emotions.

"Of course we're not, Di. Use your common sense, dear."

"All I want is for Dad to go away again," Diane went on as if her mother had not spoken. "Then Neil and I could be easy and you could marry James and be happy again. And he would have gone if only Marion hadn't given him a job on her farm."

And if I hadn't forced him to take it, Shelagh thought, by letting him see I didn't think he could do it.

But she only said curtly,

"Nonsense, Diane. I'm not unhappy."

"Yes, you are. I've heard you more than once crying in the night. And James is unhappy, too. He told me how mean you've been to him since Dad came back."

Shelagh felt a surge of real anger as the implication of her daughter's words sank in.

"Do you mean to say you've been discussing me with James?"

Diane had the grace to look slightly ashamed.

"Not really discussing you, Mom. I met him and we got talking, that's all."

"Then I'll thank you not to discuss me. Wait until I see him — "

"I knew you were against me, Mom, and it isn't fair. When I only want you to be happy again," Diane wailed, and buried her face in her hands, weeping noisily with all the abandonment of a child.

Shelagh got up and went to her, sitting on the arm of her chair and putting her arm around her, her impatience disappearing before the realisation that however annoying Di's attitude might be, this was something which was of real importance to her.

"You know that isn't true, my dear," she said gently.

Diane sniffed miserably.

"I suppose I do. I'm sorry, Mom, but everything's gone wrong. Neil knows now that Dad's been in prison and I didn't want him to."

"He had to know some time," Shelagh said reasonably. "I'm sure he won't mind about it too much."

"That's just it he doesn't. Oh, Mom, he was really mean to me when he heard about it, because he'd met Dad by then and he *likes* him. He thinks he's great because he isn't letting things get him down. Because he's trying to make a new career for himself."

"And isn't that a good thing?"

"No, it isn't. He thinks you and I are terrible because we don't feel the same as he does. We've had the most foul quarrel and now he won't speak to me."

She was ready to burst into tears again and Shelagh said, quickly, knowing that sympathy was the last thing to offer her if she wanted to prevent another outburst,

"That isn't the end of the world, Di. A marriage isn't real until husband and wife have a row about something. Think how boring it would be if you and Neil agreed with each other all the time."

"But this was different. Neil said Marion was quite right to tell me to go away and grow up! You'd think a husband would always take his wife's side, wouldn't you," she added indignantly. "Not some stranger's!"

Almost Shelagh was betrayed into a laugh at Diane's words, but she managed to control it.

"You should be glad he's got a mind of his own, dear," she said. "Because there are others involved in this besides you and Neil, you know, and they can be hurt, too."

Diane sighed.

"Perhaps you're right, but I still say it isn't fair to you to —

"I wish you'd remember that I'm perfectly capable of looking after myself," Shelagh interrupted tartly. "I don't need you or anyone else to do it for me. Now, you get off home and make it up with Neil. Only for heaven's sake tidy yourself up before you go, because if he sees you looking like this, he'll come round here roaring for my blood."

Diane smiled reluctantly.

"All right, Mom, if that's the way you want it."

"It is, my dear, but thank you for trying to help, even if I'm not going to let you."

Shelagh felt both physically and mentally exhausted when she came back into the room after seeing her daughter off.

She had sent her home ready to make up her first real tiff with her husband, knowing that before long everything would be all right for her again.

But she was not nearly so sure about herself. Diane had done the one thing she dreaded and she was afraid. Afraid of what Gregory's reaction would be and of her own involvement in it.

She waited for him to come home with a mounting apprehension which was not relieved even by Kate's chatter when she at last came home from her rehearsal. But as the clock moved on and he did not come, she finally went up to her room, grateful for the postponement of what she was sure would be a difficult few minutes and hoping that by morning nothing would be quite as bad as it seemed now.

But she was not given the respite for which she had hoped. She had only just got into bed when she heard a sharp rap at her door and Gregory's voice saying quietly, but with an unmistakable note of anger in it,

"Shelagh, are you awake? I must talk to you."

She did not reply at once, then as he knocked again, she got up and pulled on her dressing gown before going to open the door.

"What is it?" she asked.

"I'll tell you." His voice was quiet so as not to disturb Kate, yet the quietness seemed only to increase the menace in it. "Has Diane been here?"

"Yes."

"And did she tell you what she's had the impudence to do? She's been to Marion and told her she's no right to give me a job. That but for her I'd have had to go away, like everyone wants me to?"

"Yes, but — "

"Don't make any excuses for her, Shelagh. Because she's done the unforgivable thing. She told Marion to her face that everybody knew that she and I were lovers!"

"Gregory, I'm sorry — "

"And so you should be, because it's all your fault."

"How can you say that," she cried, and was ashamed to hear the quiver in her voice. "Why do you always blame me?"

"Why? Because you tried and

sentenced me before ever the law did! No wonder my children are all against me, too."

"That isn't true!"

Suddenly she could not bear it any longer. She had been through so much that day, was feeling physically and emotionally exhausted, and this final accusation broke the control she had tried to keep over her fears.

"I hate you for saying that, Gregory!" she cried. "I wish I'd never seen you again."

She turned away and went back into the room, flinging herself on her bed and letting the tears which she had kept in check for so long run unheeded down her cheeks.

He stood where she had left him, appalled by her sudden breakdown. Then forgetting the ban she had imposed on him, he went purposefully to her, sitting on the edge of the bed and putting his arm around her.

"Shelagh, don't cry like this. I didn't mean it. I'm sorry."

He lifted her up and held her against him, his hand pressing her head into the hollow of his shoulder. For a moment she resisted, then as a wave of despair swept over her, she relaxed against him, knowing only that she needed the comfort of his nearness, of his hands on her.

She felt his lips against her temples and cheek and turned blindly towards him.

"Gregory, I'm so unhappy. So mixed up. I don't know what to do — "

Then the words were stilled as he kissed her, hard and passionately, and all the pent up desire, the longing and frustrations of the past months flooded over her, so that all she was aware of was his nearness and her own need.

11

WHEN Shelagh awoke next morning she lay for a while, feeling drowsy and quietly content, still in that no-man's land between sleeping and waking before the body takes up the daily task again. Then she remembered, and immediately that peace was gone.

She turned her face into the pillows, appalled by what had happened; by her own weakness. She had been so sure that everything was over between herself and Gregory, that never again would she want him as a husband. And even while she tried to convince herself that it meant nothing to her, had not altered her resolve in any way, she knew it was not true.

Because Gregory would think now and, she admitted honestly, with reason, that all the misunderstandings between them were over.

He would be sure, she told herself, forgetting all her doubts about him and Marion, that they could begin to rebuild their marriage as he had wanted them to when he had first come home. It was not going to be easy to make him understand that what had happened had been the result, not of love, but of a combination of despair and uncertainty. A need for comfort and reassurance.

She moved restlessly against the pillows, sorry that once again she would have to disappoint him. Because in spite of her natural regret that their marriage was dying, she was still sure she did not want to live again through the unhappiness and frustration she had known over the past years.

"Mom, it's nearly eight o'clock. Aren't you getting up? Are you all right?"

Kate's voice roused her from her thoughts and she sat up quickly, glad of the interruption.

"Yes, of course, dear. I must have overslept. I'll be right down."

"Shall I start the breakfast?"

"Yes, please, Kate."

She got out of bed and pulled on her dressing gown, feeling reluctant to go downstairs and face up to the difficulties which were crowding in on her, yet glad that Kate's need of her was forcing her to overcome that weakness.

It was only when she reached the door that she saw the letter lying on the floor.

She picked it up and unfolded it, a pulse beginning to beat nervously in her throat. Then she caught her breath sharply, hardly able to believe what she was reading.

Because she had been quite wrong. Gregory had not misunderstood after all. He made it quite clear that what had happened between them last night was only an episode, and one to be deplored and not repeated.

"I'm sorry," he had written. "I

wouldn't have had that happen for anything, especially now. But don't worry. It won't ever be repeated. Marion has offered me a cottage at the farm and I'm going to accept. She says she'll make sure I don't starve, and maybe this move will solve all our problems."

She stared down at it, seeing the words 'especially now' and 'this will solve all our problems' dancing in front of her eyes. What did he mean by them?

But even as she asked herself that question, she knew the answer. He was making it quite clear to her that since he had met Marion he no longer wanted to rebuild their marriage. That he saw this move to the farm as the ending of their life together, and the beginning of a new one with Marion.

Everything was finished then, she thought despondingly. Twenty years of marriage ended as if it had never been. That was what she had wanted, yet now it had come she felt a sick wave of depression and pain sweep through her.

"Mom! Aren't you coming? Breakfast's ready."

She thrust the letter into her pocket and forced herself to open the door and walk downstairs, straightening her shoulders consciously before going into the kitchen where Kate was already eating her breakfast.

The need to hide this crisis from her young daughter, to appear as usual, helped her to recover in some measure from the shock of the letter, and gave her the excuse to shelve for the time being the decision she would soon have to make.

Yet in the end it was Kate who finally made her face up to the truth. "Don't forget I'll be late tonight," she warned as she set out for school. "We've got another rehearsal of the choir. Oh, Mom, I am glad Dad's come home in time to be there. It'll be great having you both this year. It'll make all the difference. See you, love."

Shelagh watched her cycle away and knew that, at whatever cost to herself, she could not spoil Kate's happiness in having her father back. Not yet, at least. When the concert was over, when she had had time to prepare her for the inevitable parting, then she would welcome the break which had to be accepted one day.

It was not going to be easy to ask Gregory to come back home, even though it was for a short time, but she was sure he would do it for Kate's sake. And with that decision made she was aware of a lessening of the tension which had been increasing within her ever since she had awakened that morning.

She was still of the same mind when she left the shop earlier than usual and went home. She went at once to the shed and wheeled out Diane's old bicycle, bending her head against the thin cold wind which had sprung up as she set out for the farm.

It was only as she walked hesitantly into the yard that she felt the first doubts, realised clearly the difficulty of the task she had undertaken.

Because even if she was able to find Gregory without making her presence known to anyone else at the farm, it was not going to be an easy task to ignore last night and ask him to come back home, even though it was for Kate's sake.

She turned quickly towards the stable as the door opened, feeling her heart begin to pound heavily, and was aware of a sense of disappointment and dismay when she saw Marion come through it.

She stopped, looking at Shelagh in surprise.

"What do you want?"

"I've come to see Gregory."

Shelagh was relieved to find her voice quiet and firm, betraying none of the perturbation she felt at this first setback to her plans.

Then as Marion walked towards her,

the dismay gave way to an unwilling admiration. Gregory was right, she told herself wryly. In riding breeches and cream shirt, open to show the strong column of her throat, Marion looked regal and almost beautiful, making Shelagh herself feel untidy and, somehow, quite unimportant.

"What do you want Gregory for?" she asked.

"I have to talk to him."

She looked up at the other woman, meeting her gaze proudly, sure now that she was perfectly well aware of why she wanted to talk to Gregory, certain that she would do everything she could to prevent that happening.

Then to her intense surprise, Marion said abruptly,

"He's working the four acre field."

"Thank you. I'll go up there — "

Marion put out a detaining hand.

"Don't go yet. He won't run away. There's enough work to be done to keep him occupied all day. I'd like to talk to you first."

"I don't think we have anything to say to each other, Marion," Shelagh said quietly.

"We have, though the yard isn't the best place. Come into the house, will you?"

Shelagh hesitated, knowing that the last thing she wanted at that moment was a showdown with Marion. Then as the other woman walked purposefully towards the house, she shrugged and followed her. As well to get it over now, she thought fatalistically. At least she would be under no illusions when she at last talked to Gregory.

"Well, what is it?" she asked, standing just inside the kitchen door.

Marion looked at her consideringly.

"Don't you know?"

"No. How should I?"

"Then I'll tell you. I think it's time you and I came to an understanding."

"In what way?"

"Don't fence with me, Shelagh." Marion's voice was impatient. "You know well enough what I mean. How

212

much longer do you intend to cling to Gregory?"

Shelagh flushed.

"I don't cling, as you term it. He's my husband and — "

"I'm glad you remember it, even if it is only when it suits you. You make me tired! You're so lucky to be married to a man like Gregory, and you haven't the sense to appreciate it."

"What makes you think I haven't?"

"You're not going to deny it, are you? Why, you haven't even the most elementary loyalty of a true wife."

"What do you mean by that?"

"As if you don't know," Marion said scornfully. "Didn't you judge him and find him guilty long before any court of law did?"

"No! I didn't."

"Then why did you pretend he'd deserted you instead of telling everyone that even though he had been sent to prison, you still believed in him?"

"It was for the children," Shelagh said painfully.

Marion looked at her.

"Yes, you're a mother first and a wife a long way after, aren't you? You ought to consider — one day your children will all go away and you'll be left alone."

Shelagh did not reply, feeling helpless in the face of the other's contempt, and Marion went on,

"But you won't, will you? I'd forgotten for the moment. You're planning to marry again. James Seaton, isn't it? Though how you can even look at him after knowing Gregory! You must be crazy!"

Shelagh clenched her hands into fists, determined not to give Marion the satisfaction of knowing how much she had hurt her, trying to speak coolly and quietly but not really succeeding as she said unsteadily,

"I can't see what business it is of yours what I do."

"Can't you? Then I'll tell you. I love Gregory. I want to make him happy, to give him all the things he's missed out on in the last few years, through you and Brian and Diane."

Shelagh drew in her breath sharply.

"How dare you talk to me like this!"

"Of course I dare. So would any woman who really loves her man. But you wouldn't understand that," she added bitingly. "You don't know what it is to love without thought of yourself."

"And you do, I suppose?"

"I think so. Look, Shelagh," she went on urgently, "you don't really want Gregory. Why won't you let him go?"

"So that you can have him?"

"Yes, if he wants me. I've no false pride. I'll go to him any time he says the word, with or without marriage."

"You can't mean that!"

"Why not? I don't mind what people say or think about me — "

"But what about Gregory?" Shelagh interposed quickly. "Have you thought of him?"

"Yes. That's why I'm asking you to give him his freedom."

Shelagh looked at her, feeling trapped and helpless in the face of Marion's single-minded purpose, wishing she could hurt her as she herself had been hurt by her words.

"What makes you think Gregory will want you on any terms?" she asked sharply, and was immediately sorry when she saw Marion's mouth tighten with pain.

"He may not," she answered quietly. "I don't know because he's too fine a man to two-time his wife. But I'm willing to take that risk. So what's your answer, Shelagh?"

"Why should I do what you want?"

"Oh, why don't you grow up?" Marion said impatiently. "You're like a dog with a bone. You don't want Gregory yourself but you won't let anyone else have him either. Especially someone who loves him and only wants to make him as happy as he deserves to be."

"Why, you — you — "

The words she wanted to say caught in her throat and Shelagh turned away blindly, trying to control the rush of tears which stung behind her eyes.

Then as Marion began to speak again she almost ran from the house, intent only on getting away from this woman who knew what she wanted and was so determined to get it.

She heard Marion call out to her but she did not stop, not until she reached the roadway where she had left the bicycle. She picked it up but did not immediately get onto it, too disturbed to go in search of Gregory yet.

"You're like a dog with a bone. You don't want him yourself and you won't let anyone else have him."

She could hear Marion's words ringing in her ears, and her fingers tightened on the handle bars. Was that true? A short while ago she would have dismissed those words contemptuously, but now she was not nearly so sure. She was as confused about her own feelings as she was about Gregory's.

Not like Marion Black, she thought suddenly. She so obviously had no doubts at all. And she was aware of an unwilling admiration for her because she knew what she wanted and had the courage to go out and fight for it.

And as she at last got onto the bicycle and began to cycle towards the four acre field she knew that the clear cut objective with which she had started out had become blurred and altered. That beneath the wish not to hurt her young daughter there was now another desire and one which at that moment her mind refused to either recognise or analyse.

All she was sure of now was that there was no longer any certainty that Gregory would do as she wanted him to, for Kate's sake.

Because if Marion was right, and surely she had spoken from a knowledge of his heart, even though she seemed to be unsure, then not even the happiness of his daughter would count for anything with him.

And at that thought Shelagh was aware again of a feeling of depression and frustration deeper and more painful than anything she had experienced up to now.

12

THE certainty of failure was still with Shelagh as she reached the four acre field, a certainty which chilled her heart as completely as the biting wind chilled her body.

She dismounted from the cycle and laid it down on the grass verge, rubbing her hands and legs, trying to bring some life back into them.

Far across the field she could see a tractor running busily backwards and forwards, and strained her eyes to see if it was Gregory who was driving it, but it was too far away for her to be sure.

She huddled into her coat, waiting impatiently for the machine to make its way towards her, feeling a sick sense of disappointment when she saw that it was not Gregory after all.

"Where's Mr. Muir?" she called

when it came closer to her, and had to repeat the question before the elderly farm hand heard her.

"He's gone back to the farm this half hour, ma'am, and I'm going to follow him. It's getting too cold for an old 'un like me to be out now. And for you, too. You look fair perished, m'dear."

"I'm all right. I'll go after him. Thank you," she said, and bent once more to pick up the bicycle, thinking dispiritedly as she went back the way she had come that everything seemed to be conspiring against her that day.

Though the thought did not make her deviate from her intention. Because she knew that if she did not see Gregory that day, by tomorrow it would be too late. She would have lost the sense of urgency, of dedication almost, which was driving her on in spite of everything.

From the roadway above the farm she saw him come out of the barn and walk across to the house, his figure plainly illuminated by the light from the kitchen as he opened the door and went inside. Then the darkening twilight, broken only by the light streaming from the window, took over again.

She dismounted quickly and laid the bicycle down at the side of the road, then walked down the path in the gathering darkness, determined to wait outside the house until he came out again.

Cautiously she approached the lighted window, not wanting to be seen by those within, but she need not have worried. The two standing so close together in the middle of the kitchen had eyes for nobody but each other.

As she watched, Gregory laid his hand for a moment on Marion's hair, then pulled her head against his shoulder, holding her closely against him so that her face was hidden from the watcher at the window.

They stood for a while, then he bent his head and put his lips against her hair.

Shelagh turned away sharply, unable

to look any longer, sure now that her mission was quite hopeless. Marion had seemed to be unsure of Gregory's love for her, but Shelagh now had no doubts. His love had been plainly visible for anyone to see.

And as she began the journey home, she was aware of a coldness within her which had nothing to do with the wind which numbed her face and hands.

Inside the warm kitchen Gregory looked up sharply, attracted by Shelagh's sudden movement without realising what had disturbed him. Marion stirred against him.

"What's the matter, Gregory?" she asked.

"Nothing. I thought I saw something — at the window — "

He broke off as the telephone began to ring insistently.

"There's the phone. I'll answer it, shall I?"

She put up her hand to deter him.

"No, leave it. Let it ring."

He put her gently from him.

"I can't, my dear. It might be something urgent, I won't be a minute."

She watched him go out of the kitchen, knowing that the moment, so magical yet so bitter sweet, had gone, yet still clinging to the hope that Gregory's impulse to comfort her when he found her unhappy and disturbed after Shelagh's visit meant that he was at last beginning to love her.

But that hope was shattered as soon as he came back into the kitchen, looking very worried.

"I've got to go home, Marion," he said quickly. "It was Kate on the phone. She's alone in the house and in a real tizzy because Shelagh hasn't come home."

Marion felt the colour surge into her face at his words but before she could make up her mind whether or not to tell him about Shelagh's call at the farm, he went on,

"Kate rang the shop and Dorothy said she'd left early saying she was going straight home. I'll have to go.

I can't leave Kate alone. See you, my dear."

She followed him to the door, watching him stride away from her without a backward look, standing without movement until she heard the engine of the jeep start into life and watched its lights disappear round the bend at the top of the hill.

Then she shivered uncontrollably and went back indoors, feeling lonely and bereft, facing up to the truth. The truth that whatever had happened over the past years, the ties of his marriage, the needs of his wife and children, were still of paramount importance to him. Of greater importance, she admitted sadly to herself, than she could ever be, however deeply he might value her help and friendship.

She went to the telephone, knowing that she should have told Gregory that Shelagh had been looking for him, but even as she stretched out her hand to lift the receiver, her mood changed. She was reading too much into his concern. Of course he would rush off following Kate's plea for help, but that did not necessarily have the meaning she was placing on it.

Because that was the kind of thing she would do herself. Had done times without number when somebody had appealed to her for help.

She went back into the kitchen and sat down by the stove. She would give him time to get home, then ring and find out if Shelagh had arrived. If not, then it would be time enough to tell him what she knew. And having made that decision she felt once again more hopeful and optimistic, looking forward to a time in the future when she and Gregory would be happy together at last.

★ ★ ★

It seemed a lifetime to Shelagh before she reached home, and by the time she had dismounted from the bicycle and put it away she was shaking uncontrollably.

She closed the door of the shed behind her and groped her way to the kitchen door, hardly knowing what she was doing.

Kate jumped up from the chair by the stove in which she had been huddled and ran over to her, her face lighting up and losing its pinched look.

Then when she really looked at her mother all the worry of the past hour surged back again.

"Mom, what's happened to you? Where've you been?" she said, putting her arm around Shelagh and helping her to the chair which she had just vacated. "I've been worried to death about you. Are you feeling ill?"

Hearing the note almost of panic in her young daughter's voice, Shelagh made a real effort and smiled up at her.

"No, love. I'm cold, that's all. I'll be all right when I've had a hot drink. Make some tea for me, will you, dear?"

"Right ho. The kettle's on the boil so it won't be a minute," she said, relieved at having something definite to do. "I'll make enough for the three of us. I expect Dad will be glad of a cup when he comes, too."

Shelagh closed her eyes, seeing clearly Gregory and Marion in each other's arms, feeling a pain which was almost physical at that remembrance.

"He won't be coming for a long time, Kate," she said, with an effort. "He'll be too busy at the farm."

Kate turned round in surprise.

"Yes, he will. He said he'd come right away when I rang him."

"You rang him?" Shelagh echoed. "What for, Kate?"

Kate switched off the kettle and poured the boiling water into the teapot before she said,

"I was worried about you, Mom. I rang Dorothy, too, and she said you'd left the shop ages ago and were coming straight home. So I rang Dad — "

"Kate, you shouldn't have done that,"

Shelagh said, seeing again Gregory and Marion so lost in each other, so evidently happy together.

"Why not? Dad didn't mind. He said he'd come over right away. And here he is," she added with relief as the door was thrust open and Gregory came quickly in. "She's home, Dad. She's just come."

"Are you all right, Shelagh?" He looked down at her, then put his hand over hers. "You're frozen to the bone. Kate, put some water on to boil for hot bottles while I get the brandy."

"Right ho. I'm glad you've come, Dad. I didn't know just what to do."

While she was away he chafed Shelagh's cold hands, but so impersonally that she was never under any illusion about him. He was doing for her what he would have done for anyone under such circumstances, and while she was grateful to him, she was also aware of a depth of sadness which made her feel even more weary and dispirited than she had been.

When Kate came back he poured out the brandy and held it to her lips, but she took it from him, and sipped it, her teeth chattering against the glass. The neat spirit made her cough, but she was grateful for the tiny oasis of warmth which it brought to her chilled body.

Gregory filled the bottles competently, and when they were ready said quietly,

"You'd better get right into bed, Shelagh. Kate will bring the tea up when you're ready, and I'll give you a tablet to take."

She got up at once, struggling to her feet, then putting out her hand gropingly as the room moved crazily round her.

She felt herself lifted off her feet and knew that Gregory was carrying her, and was glad to relax against him and let him carry her upstairs.

He went into her bedroom, apparently without any remembrance of what had happened there so recently, and put her down in the easy chair, before going downstairs again.

She stayed where he had put her, beginning to shiver again now that the warmth of his cradling arms was gone, and he looked sharply at her when he came in a few minutes later with the hot water bottles.

He pulled back the covers and put the bottles in the bed before saying gently,

"You'd better get undressed, Shelagh. You'll feel better when you're in your bed."

She got up shakily, but determined this time that she would not look to him for any help and began to undress with clumsy, still numb fingers.

He watched her for a moment then with an impatient exclamation came to her aid, stripping off her clothes quickly and competently and pulling her nightgown over her head.

Then he put his arm around her and helped her into bed. She relaxed as he pulled the bedclothes around her, feeling the comforting warmth beginning to seep into her, a warmth not only external, but also internal because of his kindness to her.

She drank the tea which Kate brought up a moment later, and swallowed the tablet Gregory brought for her from his own bedroom, then slid gratefully down into the bed. She smiled up into the two faces watching her.

"Thank you, both of you. I'll be fine now," she said, already feeling drowsy.

"She'll sleep now, Kate," she heard Gregory say as if from a long way off. "That tablet is pretty potent."

And as she submerged into unconsciousness, his face looking down at her was the last thing she saw. Just as it was the first thing she saw as she slowly awoke next morning.

He was asleep in the chair, the eiderdown off his own bed wrapped around him, his face relaxed and defenceless, all the bitter lines smoothed away, looking achingly like the young doctor she had married with so much love and joy.

She gazed at him, realising suddenly that this was the first time she had really seen him since he had come home, feeling a stab of nostalgic pain as she remembered, looking back down the years.

They had been so happy then, filled with love and laughter, living for each other and for those glorious moments of ecstasy and delight in the fulfilment of their love for each other.

Now it was all gone, lost to her for ever. She had known that since she had seen him and Marion together. No matter what happened in the future, she would never recapture that enchantment again. Not even if she agreed to do what James wanted her to divorce Gregory.

But even as she thought it, she knew that way out was not for her. She had always believed that marriage was for life, and it was not easy to change her mind now, at her age. For her there could be no happiness in a second marriage, even with James whom she had always been fond of.

She did not know when it first occurred to her that maybe she was being selfish. Perhaps it was the moment when Gregory stirred in the chair and sighed deeply in his sleep. It was certainly afterwards that the thought first came into her mind. That although there could be no future for herself in a second marriage, that might not be true for Gregory.

And in that moment of understanding she admitted to herself that she had no right to prevent him from finding with Marion the happiness which she herself could no longer give him. Though it was long enough before she acknowledged that if he wanted his freedom, she had no right to deny it to him because of her own beliefs; and even longer before she decided that if he asked her to do so, she would give him a divorce.

Though that decision brought with it no tranquillity of mind, but rather an intensification of the confusion which had been with her from the moment he had walked into the house on Di's wedding day. A confusion which was added to by a pang of real suffering, an almost unbearable hatred of the woman who had been given Gregory's love. Who would take her place in his life, know the ecstasy which had once been only for herself and him.

She sat up in bed and looked at him, trying to read in his face the answer to her problems, and as if feeling her gaze on him he stirred and woke, fully and completely, as he had always done.

She smiled and held out her hand to him.

"Have you been up all night, Gregory? How good you are to me."

He pushed the eiderdown onto the floor and came to her, but did not touch her outstretched hand and after a moment she let it drop again.

"How are you feeling this morning?"

"All right. A fraud really. I ought to be up and about, not lying here like this."

"No, you shouldn't. In fact, I would advise you to stay in bed today. I hope we've averted a bad chill but I can't be sure yet. If you don't feel so good during the day, I think you'd better call your doctor in."

She looked at him in surprise.

"What for, when you're looking after me?"

"You're forgetting something, aren't you?" he asked curtly. "I'm not allowed to."

She put her hand impulsively on his arm.

"I'm sorry, Gregory. I'd completely forgotten for the moment."

He lifted his hand as if to put it over hers, then thrust it deep into his pocket.

"It doesn't do to forget that kind of thing," he said, turning away. "I'll go and see about some breakfast for you."

"No, not yet. Wait a minute, Gregory."

He paused and looked round at her, his eyes wary.

236

"What is it?"

"It's — about your letter. There's no need for you to go away. I — I don't want you to"

He took a swift step back to her, his face lighting up with hope, a light which she did not see.

"You mean — do you mean — ?"

Still she did not look at him but played restlessly with the bed cover.

"You see, Kate's so happy because you've come home. I'd rather you didn't go away yet, not until I've prepared her a bit. I don't want to hurt her too badly."

He drew back, his face hardening into bitter lines again.

"So it's Kate you're worrying about. I ought to have known, I suppose."

She looked at him then, hearing a note in his voice which she found disturbing, but already he had his emotions under control, so that she did not see the expression of pain which had momentarily twisted his mouth.

"I don't understand you," she said,

with a puzzled frown. "What do you mean?"

"Nothing. Leave it, Shelagh."

"Will you come then? It need only be for a short while."

"I suppose so, though I'm not only thinking of Kate. There's Marion as well, you know."

"Marion?" she asked, and was surprised by the stab almost of jealousy at his words.

"Yes. While I was working the four acre field today I had plenty of time to think. I can't take that cottage she offered to me because people are bound to talk, so I decided I'd look for lodgings — if anyone will have me. But now you've saved me the trouble."

"I see" she said slowly.

"I'm glad you do. Marion doesn't care what people say or think, so I've got to be doubly careful. I must protect her reputation as much as I can."

"Yes." She stopped, knowing that the moment she had waited for had come, that now she was going to find out the truth. And suddenly she was so afraid of his answer that she could hardly say the words. "Gregory, are you — do you love her,"

He frowned down at her.

"Why? What does it matter to you?"

"That's a silly question — " she began.

"Is it? Because you're hoping it's true, so that you can marry James?" he interposed swiftly. "Well, I've no objection as long as you remember one thing. You're not getting a divorce at Marion's expense. I'll supply the evidence whenever you want it, but leave her out of your plans."

"But I don't want it!" she cried, and was answered only by the sound of the door closing decisively behind him.

"Gregory!" she called again, but he did not come back, and after a moment she sank wearily against the pillows, staring blindly at the door, torn and shaken by the emotions which surged within her.

Though it was a while before she

admitted the truth which she found so difficult to face. That the deep pain she felt was caused by jealousy — jealousy of Marion who had been lucky enough to gain Gregory's love.

Only now, when she had lost him, when it was too late, did she understand her own heart and acknowledge with despair that she still loved him.

Not perhaps with the unquestioning devotion she had given him in those first years of marriage, but with a love quieter and more mature, deeper and less selfish and demanding. Because at last she had grown up and could accept that he, like other people, had faults as well as virtues. That whatever he might have done in the past, she could and must forgive him because of her love for him.

And now she had lost him, through her own stupidity, and in that bitter moment she knew that without him her life would be purposeless and barren, without joy or meaning.

Marion was right, she thought drearily.

She had been a fool, a crazy fool to throw away the love which had been hers for the taking. She knew now when it was too late.

She had sent him away and he had gone — to Marion. He had fallen in love with her and now did not want her, Shelagh, any more. She was no longer necessary to him except that, without her help, he would never be able to marry as she knew he must want to.

That was the one thing now that she could do for him. Give him his freedom if that was what he wanted. Though it was a long time before she could overcome the desire to hold on in the hope that one day he would turn back to her, but in the end she won that bitter victory.

She closed her eyes knowing that this was going to be the most difficult task she had faced in her life. Then she covered her face with her hands, praying that she might be given the strength to carry it out without flinching.

13

SHELAGH sat up eagerly as the bedroom door opened, then sank back again, ashamed of her disappointment when she saw it was Kate who was coming in carrying a tray carefully and not Gregory.

"I've brought you your breakfast, Mom," she said cheerfully. "Dad says you're to stay in bed today."

"Thank you, dear, but oughtn't you to have gone to school? You'll be very late."

"I thought I'd stay till I'd seen you in case you wanted me to stay at home. Do you, Mom?"

"Of course not, Kate. I'll be all right. There's really nothing the matter with me. Where is your father?" she added as casually as she could.

"He's gone to the farm. He was madly late, but he said Marion wouldn't mind."

No, Shelagh thought, wryly, Marion certainly would not mind. Why should she when she had won out all along the line?

"Are you going to the shop, Mom?"

"Perhaps, later on. You get off to school now, Kate. There's no need for you to stay at home for me."

"Right ho, if you're sure you'll be all right. Dad said I'd — "

"Of course I will," she interrupted, and was glad when Kate went out and she was alone again.

She got up as soon as she had drunk the coffee her daughter had brought, though she did not eat any of the food, feeling at that moment incapable of swallowing it, but she could not settle in the house. There were too many regrets, too much sadness to be borne alone, and before long she left the house and walked through the village to the shop.

Dorothy came to meet her as she went in.

"You're late, Mrs. Muir. I was beginning to get worried. Are you all right? You don't look so good."

"Weary, that's all, Dorothy. These past weeks have been hectic, but there's nothing else wrong with me. How's trade today?"

"Back to normal, thank goodness. In fact, I'm glad you have come in because I think we're going to have one of those days."

She was right about that and Shelagh was thankful. Apart from the relief of knowing that the boycott was apparently over, she was glad to be kept busy because it helped to keep her mind off her own tangled affairs.

She was closing the shop doors after the last lingering customer when she saw James crossing the road towards her.

She had an involuntary desire to slam the door shut and lock it, loth to talk to him today, and it was an effort not to do so. Instead she held the door open welcomingly.

"Shelagh, you look exhausted, my dear." He took her hand in his, his eyes worried. "I wish you wouldn't work so hard."

"Hard work never killed anyone, so they say," she answered quickly, pulling her hand away from his. "We have had a busy day, I'm glad to say, and I suppose it's tired me a bit more than usual because of last night."

"What happened last night?"

"Oh, I just got thoroughly chilled. Gregory said I ought to stay in bed today in case there were any ill effects, but I didn't want to."

He frowned at her words.

"Gregory? He isn't doctoring you, surely?"

"Of course not," she said quickly, annoyed with herself for giving him the opportunity to ask that question. "Or not more than any husband would if his wife wasn't feeling very well."

He sighed, looking suddenly old and defeated, then put his hands on her shoulders, turning her to face him.

"Shelagh, I don't understand you lately. You've changed. You're not the same person"

"But that's ridiculous, James."

"It isn't. Shelagh, I've got to know," he said urgently, his fingers tightening painfully. "I can't go on any longer in this state of suspense. Are you ever going to break finally with Gregory? Is there any hope for me?"

"We can't talk about it here, James. Somebody may come. Dorothy is still in the shop. Let's leave it till tomorrow."

"No. I've got to know now, Shelagh," he said firmly. She hesitated a moment longer, then shrugged off his retaining hands.

"All right. Come up to the office then."

He followed her up the stairs, and did not say anything until he closed the office door behind them. Then he said quietly,

"Well, Shelagh? What's your answer? Please tell me the truth, darling."

He sounded so humble, so unlike his

usual dogmatic self that she was more touched than she would have been if he had tried to bulldog an answer from her.

"You know I will, James," she said. "I've asked Gregory to give me a divorce."

His eyes lit up, all the unhappiness gone at once from his bearing.

"But that's wonderful, Shelagh!"

He went to her, taking her in his arms and pulling her close against him. She felt his lips on hers and knew a moment of real revulsion, a desperate desire to push him away, and was forced to hold that reaction rigidly in check.

"Yes, I suppose so," she said tepidly.

He looked at her sharply. "You're pleased, aren't you? What's wrong, my dear?"

She broke away from him, irrationally annoyed at his final words, at his failure to recognise what this step must mean to her.

"It's not the easiest thing in the

world, to get a divorce — "

He laughed buoyantly.

"It is in this case! The evidence is there for everyone to see. He and Marion Black are known — "

"No," she interrupted sharply. "You can't cite Marion!"

"Don't be silly, Shelagh. Of course we can."

"We can't," she said again. "If we do, Gregory says he will fight every inch of the way. If we don't, then he's agreed to supply the necessary evidence."

"I see. So he's trying to protect her good name. A bit late for that, I'd have thought — still, a laudable attempt. I think I'd better go and have a talk with him about this."

"No, don't, please!"

He looked at her in surprise.

"Why not? This affects me as well as you, Shelagh. It's my prerogative to take charge of everything. Surely you understand that?"

She sat down in the chair beside the

desk, trying to think of some way of making him understand that for him to go and see Gregory might ruin everything, and was surprised at the sudden elation which surged through her at that thought.

Though she was glad to remember afterwards that it was not this which made her cease to resist James's plan, but rather the knowledge that nothing she could say would ever make him change his mind once he had made a decision.

"Do just as you think right," she said at last.

"I will. You can leave it all to me. Don't worry any longer, my dearest."

He pulled her to her feet again, holding her hands tightly in his.

"Thank you," she said and was ashamed of the lack of enthusiasm in her voice. But he did not seem to notice anything amiss, and went on exultingly,

"Shelagh, darling, I can't believe that things are coming right for us at last, after all these years. I'll make you so happy, my dearest dear."

His hands slid up her arms and his mouth came down on hers, hard and demanding, and she let him have his way, too heartsick to protest any longer, hoping that in his own passion he would not notice that her response to his love-making was almost non-existent.

After a while he held her away from him and smiled down at her.

"I love you so much, my dearest," he said tenderly. "I think I've always loved you, ever since you were a very small girl. I can hardly believe we'll be able to get married at last. I've waited so long for you, darling."

She knew a moment's panic at his words and said urgently, "James, don't — I can't"

She stopped, not knowing how to tell him that he was taking too much for granted. That even if she gave Gregory his freedom, she did not want to marry again.

Then as she saw the happy light in his eyes, she knew she could not say those words.

"You can't what?" he asked.

She sighed.

"Nothing, James."

"Good." He laughed with relief. "For a moment I thought you were going to jilt me again, as you did all those years ago. A silly thought, because everything's different now, isn't it?"

"Yes," she said, and knew that what he said was the truth.

Because she could never tell him now that she did not love him, could never love him, when she had given him so much cause to think otherwise over the past few months.

She would have to go through with it to the bitter end and, after all, what would it matter to her when she had lost Gregory? There could be no happiness for her in the future, but perhaps in trying to make James happy she might find for herself some measure of contentment.

"I'll go and see Gregory then," he said buoyantly, breaking in on her dismal thoughts. "I want to get the whole business settled as soon as I can. No sense in wasting any more time. I don't want to have to wait very much longer for you, my dearest love."

He kissed her again and she endured it patiently, telling herself that this was something she must get used to. Though she was deeply glad when he dropped her at her home and made no suggestion that he should go in with her.

She watched until he was out of sight, waving jauntily as he left her, looking as if he had nothing in the world left to wish for, before going into the house, feeling drained of all emotion.

Kate had not yet come home and she was glad to be alone for a while. She sat down before the unlit fire, but in a moment she was up again, moving restlessly about the room, trying to control her chaotic thoughts.

It was only gradually that she began to understand the enormity of what she had done in allowing James to go away convinced that she loved him and wanted to marry him. That she was ready and anxious to divorce Gregory for her own sake.

She stood still at that realisation, clenching her hands tightly together. "I must have been mad to contemplate doing such a thing," she told herself desperately. "To imagine even for a minute that I could marry James, when it's Gregory I love."

She sat down abruptly, feeling as if her legs would no longer support her, facing up to a self-knowledge which made her feel sick and ashamed.

She had pretended to herself that she was trying not to hurt James but she had to admit now that what she intended to do was far less kind than it would have been to make a clean break at once.

How could she ever have thought she could make him happy when she was marrying him for all the wrong reasons? He did not deserve that kind of treatment, and she knew she must get in touch with him before he went to see Gregory.

She got up quickly and went to the telephone, dialling his home number with suddenly trembling fingers.

She recognised his housekeeper's voice answering her and said anxiously,

"Could I speak to Mr. Seaton, please? It's Mrs. Muir here."

"I'm sorry, Mrs. Muir, he's gone out. He didn't stay a minute, just said he'd be back in time for dinner, but to keep it hot if he was a bit late."

"Oh!" Shelagh felt completely deflated and for a moment did not know what to say. "You don't know where he's gone, do you?"

"He said something about going to the farm, but I don't know which one, Mrs. Muir. I'm sorry."

"It's all right. I'll ring later. Goodbye." She put down the receiver, then suddenly picked it up again and dialled Deepden Farm, certain that James must have gone there.

It was only when she heard Marion's voice answering that she realised how impossible it was for her to ask for James without explaining the reason why she wanted him, why she thought he had gone there.

"Hello," Marion said again. "Who is it?"

"It's Shelagh — Shelagh Muir."

There was silence for a moment, then Marion said,

"Oh, yes. Did you want me?"

"No. That is — "

"That's a pity," Marion said deliberately. "I'd hoped you were ringing to tell me what you intend to do about Gregory. I might have known it was too much to expect you to be as straightforward as that."

Shelagh felt the colour flood into her face and was shaken by a surge of anger which, coming as it did on the heels of all the tensions and emotions of that

255

difficult day, made her suddenly ready to do battle with this woman.

"Perhaps it is," she managed to say at last, her voice sharp with resentment, "but at least I'm going to be honest with you about one thing, Marion."

"And what's that?"

"Just that I'm not going to give up Gregory without a fight, without letting him know I still love him and want him."

She banged down the receiver on the words, then stayed for a moment leaning against the table, trying to control the fit of trembling which seized her.

Then as the telephone began to ring insistently she straightened up and turned resolutely away, sure that it was Marion ringing back and determined not to answer her.

She had thrown down the gauntlet now and, having done so, she felt more at peace than she would have believed possible half an hour before, even though she had still not managed to contact James, to stop him from seeing Gregory.

Because that did not seem to matter so much now that she had made her decision. The decision that she was not going to give in tamely but intended to fight for her future happiness. To try and win back the love which she had so foolishly and thoughtlessly thrown away.

14

SHELAGH'S mood of anger-induced determination did not last long, but was soon succeeded by doubt and indecision.

It was one thing to say that she was going to fight for her husband; but suppose he did not want her? That she was no longer necessary to his happiness?

That thought remained with her all the time as she got the evening meal ready for herself and Kate, and although she tried to hide her feelings from her young daughter, she was aware of her looking at her in a pulled way, and was glad when it was time for her to go up to her own room to do her homework.

She washed the dishes and put them away, feeling restless and uneasy, wishing there was some way of finding out just what had happened between James and Gregory, even while she told herself that this was something which she would hear about soon enough.

It was at that moment that the door bell rang and she stood quite still, feeling afraid to answer it, afraid that what she would be told would be the end of all her hopes for the future.

Then she pulled herself together, and as the bell pealed out again, forced herself to go to the door and see who was there, looking with surprise and dismay at Sergeant Cross.

He smiled rather pleasantly.

"Good evening, Mrs. Muir. Is your husband in?"

"No, he isn't. He never gets home from the farm much before seven and he's later than ever tonight. You'll probably find him there."

He shook his head.

"I've already been to the farm and there's no sign of him. Mrs. Black thought he'd left for home. You're sure he hasn't arrived?"

Her fingers tightened on the door knob, as a cold wave of fear shivered through her.

"Of course I'm sure. Why should I say he wasn't at home if he was? He must be still at the farm. Where else could he be?"

"I thought you might be able to tell me that, Mrs. Muir. Has he gone away?"

"Gone away?" Shelagh was aware of an intensification of the fear within her, as if the Sergeant's words had brought her own terror into focus. "Why should he do that?"

The Sergeant looked at her keenly.

"There's a good reason, Mrs. Muir. I think perhaps I'd better come in and tell you about it."

She stepped back into the hall, holding open the door for him. "Of course. I'm sorry. I wasn't thinking."

She led the way into the sitting room and waited for the Sergeant to explain, but it was a moment before he began to speak, his keen eyes looking round as if seeking for some signs of Gregory's presence in the house.

"Well, what is it you want to tell me?" Shelagh said jerkily at last.

"Your husband attacked another man earlier this evening," he said abruptly. "Did you know that?"

"Gregory did? I don't believe it."

"I'm afraid it's true, Mrs. Muir. The man who gave me the information is a leading citizen of this town and a J.P. I've no reason to doubt his word."

Shelagh's eyes widened with sudden knowledge.

"Who was it?"

"I'm sorry, I can't tell you that."

"Then I'll make a guess. Was it Mr. Seaton?"

"Why should you think that?" he countered.

"Because — "

She stopped, seeing the trap into which she had so nearly fallen. Because if she told the sergeant the reason why James had gone to see Gregory, he would then have a motive for the attack which she was sure James would never have let him know about.

"You think your husband and Mr. Seaton might have had something to quarrel about?" Sergeant Cross asked, when she did not say any more.

"Of course not. What reason could they have?"

"You know that better than I do, Mrs. Muir. Then you can't help me?"

"No."

"Then I'll just have to keep on looking until I find him." He waited a moment, then added suddenly, "You don't seem very concerned about your husband, Mrs. Muir."

She felt the hot colour flood into her face and drew in her breath sharply.

"I don't need to be. I know he hasn't done anything he shouldn't — that he hasn't run away. Why are you hounding him like this?"

"I'm not hounding him. You're quite mistaken about that. I'm his friend. That's why I'm here."

"I'm sorry. I didn't mean that. I know how kind you've been to him. He'd never go away without telling you first."

"I'd like to think so but — you'd have no objection if I took a look at his room, just to make sure his clothes are still there?"

She hesitated before replying, loth to give him that permission. She did not want him to see that Gregory slept in what was so obviously a bachelor's room instead of the double bedroom which the sergeant probably shared so comfortably with his own wife.

Then as she saw his eyes narrow in suspicion, she knew she could not refuse his request.

"Of course I've no objection," she said. "Come up stairs. You'll find everything is still there."

She led the way to Gregory's room and opened the door, standing back confidently to allow the sergeant to go in first.

He stopped just inside the room,

then went over to the wardrobe and flung it open.

"This is quite empty, Mrs. Muir," he said quietly.

"Empty? I don't believe it!"

She went quickly into the room, hardly able to believe it was true, watching as he opened the drawers in the dressing table and tallboy.

"All cleared out. So he *has* gone. When and where, please?"

Shelagh passed her hands nervously over her face, her eyes dark with shock.

"I've told you, I don't know. He can't have gone. You've got to believe me."

She stopped, a sob catching in her throat with the words. When had he done this? Certainly before she had got up, unless he had returned during the day. But if he had done that, surely Marion would have told her? So it must have been while Kate was upstairs with her, giving her her breakfast.

But why, after he had told her he would stay at home for Kate's sake?

264

Unless he had changed his mind. Yet remembering his concern for Marion, she could not believe that.

The thoughts went round and round in her head, meaningless and jumbled, until the sergeant said sharply,

"You're sure about that? He gave you no idea he was leaving home?"

She pulled herself together with an effort, hearing the note of disbelief in his voice and knowing that she must dispel it as soon as she could.

"No. I was expecting him back tonight. I've kept his supper for him. You've got to believe me, Sergeant Cross."

He smiled then, some of the suspicion going out of his eyes.

"I do, Mrs. Muir. Don't worry."

"But I can't help worrying. Where can he be?"

"I don't know but we'll find him. If not today, then tomorrow or the next day. Then we'll know the whole truth about what really happened, won't we?"

"Yes," she answered, but when she

came back from seeing him off, she knew she could not wait for that.

She had to find out what had happened between Gregory and James and after that try to think where her husband might have gone and why he should have been prepared for a journey which, presumably, he could have known nothing about before his encounter with James.

Because although the sergeant had not admitted it, she was quite sure it was James who had accused Gregory of attacking him. And she was determined that this was one thing he was not going to be allowed to shrug off as if it was of no account, when he knew better than anyone just what such an accusation meant to a man still on probation.

Perhaps this had been his revenge because Gregory had refused to discuss the divorce with him, she thought suddenly with a thrill of hope.

And if that was the truth, then she wanted to know about it as quickly as possible, and there was only one way to find out.

Quickly she put on her coat and set out for James's home, ringing the doorbell with determination.

It seemed a long time before the door was opened, so impatient was she to speak to James.

"Tell Mr. Seaton Mrs. Muir is here to see him, please," she said almost before the door was opened fully.

The housekeeper looked at her doubtfully.

"I don't think Mr. Seaton will see you. He's not too well and said he was going to bed early."

"I think he will see me. Will you please tell him I'm here," Shelagh said quietly.

"All right, Mrs. Muir. Will you come in and I'll go and ask him."

Shelagh watched her climb the stairs, still sustained by the militancy which had been building up within her on the journey to this house, determined that she was not going to leave it without seeing James, if she had to wait all night.

She looked eagerly at the housekeeper when she came down again, but was not really surprised when she said,

"Mr. Seaton will see you, Mrs. Muir. Will you come up, please? He's in his study."

James got up when Shelagh was ushered into the room, his face unsmiling, and said coldly,

"Why have you come here, Shelagh? You know I don't like you coming to my home to see me."

"I'm sorry, but I had to," she said crisply, then as he turned away from her and sat down, she said quickly,

"What on earth's happened to your face, James? It's all bruised and swollen!"

He put up his hand to his cheek at her question.

"I bumped into a door."

She smiled suddenly.

"Are you sure it wasn't somebody's fist?"

She saw the dull red surge up into his face and knew she had scored a hit. She said, pressing on without giving him time to recover,

"It was Gregory's fist, wasn't it? Why did you tell Sergeant Cross he attacked you?"

"How do you know that! If he's told you I'll have him demoted."

"Control yourself," Shelagh said quietly. "The Sergeant didn't give you away. I knew, don't forget, that you were hoping to see Gregory, so it wasn't difficult for me to guess, was it? What happened? Where is he?"

He shrugged indifferently.

"How should I know."

"But you did meet him and talk to him?"

"Yes, but not for long. As you seem to know so well, he attacked me and — "

"Why?"

"What do you mean — why?"

"Don't fence with me, James. I know

269

my husband too well. He wouldn't have hit you without some provocation. What did you say to him?"

"A man who would injure a child and leave him to die is capable of anything, Shelagh," he answered harshly, ignoring her final question.

She flushed.

"He didn't do that!"

He stared at her in disbelief.

"You've changed your mind suddenly, haven't you?"

"No, not really. And not suddenly."

"Now you're talking in riddles," he said impatiently.

She shook her head.

"I'm not. When it first happened I didn't believe he had done such a thing. I knew that the Gregory I had married couldn't have done it. Then afterwards, when he was so strange, so unlike himself, I began to doubt. I didn't know what to think. It's only recently, since I found out he had fractured his skull, that I began to understand. That's the truth, James," she finished steadily.

He shrugged.

"It still doesn't alter the facts."

"Perhaps not, but it does excuse them." She frowned at him, determined now to make him answer the question he had evaded for so long. "Why did Gregory knock you down?"

"He didn't knock me down. He attacked me without warning or reason, and caught me a glancing blow. It was I who knocked him down — down and out," he added with satisfaction.

She took a step towards him.

"You knocked him out? Is he all right?"

"How should I know. I walked away and left him there."

"You left him? Where?" she asked, feeling a sense of real anxiety as she remembered that Gregory had apparently not been seen since.

"Up by the sheep pens."

She turned towards the door.

"Thank you. Now I know where to start looking."

271

He moved across the room towards her.

"Why are you so bothered about him? Only this afternoon you told me you loved me. You promised to marry me."

She coloured faintly at the accusation in his voice.

"I know I did, and I'm truly sorry. I should never have let you think I would marry you, but I was a coward. I'd hurt you once before like that and I thought that as I had lost Gregory, I'd marry you and try to make you happy."

He looked at her as if he could hardly believe what he had heard, then said explosively,

"You thought I'd want second best? That I'd be willing to have you on any terms? You must have gone mad, Shelagh!"

"I know it must seem like that. I'm deeply sorry, James. I know now I was quite wrong — "

"Sorry!" he interrupted. "I should think you should be. You're nothing

272

but a liar and a cheat."

"Everything you say is true," she answered quietly. "I admit it and I have no defence. I'd better go, I think." She hesitated for a moment, then took a step towards him, holding out her hand. "Goodbye, James, and please, try to forgive me if you can."

He looked at her, his lips pressed tightly together, then deliberately turned away and walked over to the window, and at last she let her hand fall against her side and went quietly out of the room.

She did not blame James for his reaction, she told herself as she closed the front door behind her. Perhaps he had behaved badly, but the fault was all on her side, because what she had intended to do was quite unforgivable.

She had been false to her husband, to James, and to herself and must bear her punishment with what fortitude she could — the loveless, lonely years which stretched so drearily in front of her.

15

BY the time she reached home it was quite dark, but she did not let that deter her from the task she had set herself.

She found her big torch, then wheeled the bicycle from the outhouse, and set out for the moor above the farm where she knew Marion Black's sheep pens were.

She left the bicycle beside the track and walked along the rough path, shining the torch in front of her, keeping going by sheer will power. Because she was afraid; first of the night rustlings and noises which she heard as she trudged along; and secondly of what she might discover when she reached the end of her journey.

Yet when she reached the pens and in the light of her torch saw no unconscious body lying stretched out in the cold dampness of the night, her relief was mixed with a feeling of disappointment.

She scouted around for a few minutes before trudging back the way she had come, acknowledging ruefully that she had been hoping that she might have demonstrated her love for Gregory by helping him to recover from the blow James had dealt him.

As if that would have made any difference, she told herself as she got stiffly onto the bicycle again. Nothing now could give her back the love she had lost through her own stupidity. She would have to accept in future that it was no longer her privilege to worry about him at all.

But that, as she soon found out, was easier said than done. Almost before the thought had flashed through her mind, she was thinking about him again, wondering what could have happened to him.

Because if he was not up at the sheep pens, and not at home, then where was he? The farm was the most likely place, she knew, yet Sergeant Cross had been there and had not found him.

Yet Marion must have known where he was. However reluctantly, Shelagh had to acknowledge that Gregory would never have gone away without telling her where he was going.

It was this conviction which impelled her to get off the bicycle and walk down the road to the farm, determined to see Marion and find out what had happened to Gregory and if he was all right.

The light was shining from the uncurtained kitchen window, and she paused outside, looking into the bright room. Then she moved back quickly into the shadows at the side.

She stood quietly, unable to stop looking even though what she saw was so deeply painful to her. Gregory was sitting in a chair beside the table on which was a bowl and a first aid box, and as she watched she saw Marion gently bathe his head and face with water from the bowl.

She held on hard to the window sill, seeing his eyes alight with a blazing excitement which was recognisable even at that distance.

She could not see Marion's face, but she did not really need to. It was enough to watch the tender way in which she ministered to him, and stroked back the wet black hair from his forehead.

It was an effort to turn away at last and leave that warm inviting light, and as she went slowly home she was sick at heart, acknowledging now that all hope was gone. That Marion had won.

That had been obvious from the moment she had seen the empty drawers and wardrobe in his room. She had known then, although she had refused to admit it, that in spite of his promise to her he had changed his mind. He had packed and gone to Marion, just as it was to her he had turned for help after his quarrel with James.

She put the bicycle away and went into the living room, glad that Kate was still upstairs doing her homework, knowing that she needed to be alone for a little while to try to recover from the many shocks of that evening.

She sat down beside the fire, staring into it, looking back over the years of her life with Gregory, recognising now that although there had been difficult times, mostly she had been happy and content.

"Hi, Mom!"

She roused herself as Kate came in, not wanting her to see how worried she was, though she was not entirely successful, as her daughter's next words indicated.

"Are you all right? You look terrible," she said, with all the unthinking honesty of the young.

"I'm just a bit tired, that's all. Today's been quite something," she answered, with a smile which, while not exactly gay, seemed to set Kate's mind at ease.

"I'll make the supper, shall I?" she asked. "let's have it here, by the fire."

"All right, love. There's plenty of food in the fridge for sandwiches."

She sat quietly, purposely trying not to think at all, until Kate came back, with a tray piled high with food.

"Heavens!" she said, looking at the contents of the tray. "Who do you think you're feeding? The hungry five thousand?"

"Do you think it's too much? I did enough for Dad as well, in case he comes back. He's late tonight, isn't he?"

For a moment Shelagh could not answer, then she said stiffly,

"Yes. I expect he's been delayed by something at the farm. You can cover what's left with a cloth and leave it for him."

"Right ho, I'll do that," Kate said happily, and Shelagh was glad that she had told that small lie.

There was time enough for Kate to discover that her father had left them for good. Tomorrow she would tell her, she thought, then she would have the whole day to get used to the idea. Not spend the dark watches of the night in regrets and unhappiness.

Kate stretched and got up when she had done justice to the food she had brought in.

"Glory, was I hungry!" she said. "You didn't eat much though, Mom."

"You were so busy eating yourself, you didn't notice how much I got through."

"Maybe. I'll take these out and cover them up for Dad, then wash up. I've still some homework to finish."

"Don't sit up too late," Shelagh said automatically.

"I won't. Night, Mom. If Dad comes back soon, ask him to come up and say goodnight to me."

"I will, dear," Shelagh said, and was glad again that she had not told her daughter that night.

She sat on after Kate had gone, her mind going over and over the events of that day. Then at last she covered her face with her hands, longing for the comfort of tears to release the pent-up emotions which were slowly destroying her.

But even that comfort was denied her, and she faced the lonely future with dry eyes and deep unhappiness, so lost in her despair that she did not hear the sitting room door open, so that Gregory's unexpected question sent a shock of disbelief through her.

"Shelagh! What's the matter?"

She snatched her hands away from her face and got up quickly, almost in the same movement, looking up into Gregory's anxious eyes.

"It's you!"

"Of course it's me. Who else? Shelagh, what's wrong?" he asked again.

"Nothing, only Gregory — "

"Good. I thought for a minute you were crying."

She pulled herself together with an almost visible effort, fear for him making her hardly aware of what she was saying.

"What have you come back for?" she asked urgently. "You can't stay here. You've got to get away — "

She saw his face change, the excitement she had first noticed in the kitchen at Deepden Farm dying out of it.

"I might have known you'd change your mind," he said bitterly. "But don't worry! I've changed mine, too, since this morning — "

She looked at him, puzzled by his words, then as his meaning slowly dawned on her she put her hand urgently on his arm.

"No, I don't mean that. It's the Sergeant. He's looking for you."

He stared at her.

"What are you talking about?"

"The Sergeant. He went up to your room to see if you'd taken your clothes. They weren't there."

"Of course they weren't. I'd packed — when I thought I was going to live in Marion's cottage. I've brought them back with me, only now — why did Sergeant Cross come here?"

"Because of James."

"That fellow. I might have known. Do you know what he had the impudence to do, Shelagh?"

She nodded.

"Yes. He told me he'd been to see you, that he'd knocked you down."

"He did nothing of the kind! I knocked him down, I'm glad to say. Then when he scrambled to his feet, he took a swipe at me and I side-stepped and tripped over a stone I hadn't noticed. I gave my head one hell of a crack," he added, rubbing it ruefully. "I was out for the count, dead to the world!"

"And he walked away and left you lying there," she said bitterly. "Then went and told Sergeant Cross you'd attacked him without any reason."

"So that's why he's looking for me."

"Yes. Gregory, you've got to go away until this blows over."

"Nonsense. I've no reason to run away, and I'm certainly not going to let James drive me away." He looked down at her frowningly, then went on slowly, "I know it isn't any of my business what you do, Shelagh, and you'll probably tell me so, but I wish you'd believe me. That man's dangerous. He came at me like a madman. Think carefully before you do anything irrevocable."

"Like marrying him?"

He looked at her quickly, puzzled by the note in her voice.

"Yes," he said heavily.

She smiled then, a travesty of a smile devoid of mirth.

"You needn't worry, Gregory. I've no intention of marrying him, no matter what happens."

He took a quick step towards her.

"Do you mean that?"

"Yes. Once I thought I could but now — " She shivered suddenly, uncontrollably. "I know I couldn't bear it."

He came closer to her, taking her chin in his fingers, forcing her to look at him.

"Why couldn't you?" he asked quietly.

She tried to turn her head away from his compelling gaze but he held her firmly, and asked again,

"Why couldn't you?"

She closed her eyes, knowing that now there must be complete honesty between them. That although she had lost him, she had to let him know she still loved him.

Only she could not bear to look at him while she told him.

"Because I know now it's you I love, Gregory."

He was silent for so long, standing holding her without moving, that she opened her eyes and looked at him anxiously, wondering why he did not speak.

"Even though I've been gaoled for leaving that child to die?" he said at last.

"Yes. It doesn't matter what you've

done in the past. I know that now. I've been a fool, Gregory. Somehow I lost the way." She tried to smile, her eyes glittering with unshed tears. "But don't worry. I'm not going to make a nuisance of myself. I'll give you your freedom so that you can marry Marion."

He smiled down at her.

"You're very anxious to get rid of me, aren't you?"

"No." Her breath caught on the word of denial. "Only when I'd been up to the sheep pens to look for you — "

"You went to look for me?"

"Yes. After the Sergeant went I called at James's house and made him tell me where he'd left you. But you weren't there."

"I came round pretty quickly and walked back to the farm."

"I know. I saw you there — with Marion. That's when I decided I wouldn't stand in your way if you want a divorce, Gregory."

"But I don't want a divorce," he said almost violently.

She looked at him, a dawning hope in her eyes.

"You don't? Why?"

"Because whatever you may think, Shelagh, it's you I love. You and only you. Is there any hope, darling? Can we begin again?"

"Oh, yes, please," she breathed and there was no more need for words as his mouth came down on hers, their kisses dispelling the unhappiness and despair of the past weeks.

Then at last he said quietly,

"Are you sure, Shelagh?"

"Quite sure," she said steadily.

"In spite of everything?"

"Because of everything." She was silent again, then said with a smile, "And to think that in the end it was James who gave you back to me. Poor James."

"Poor James indeed!" he said indignantly. "I'm only sorry I knocked myself out before I beat him to a jelly!

But no! What am I talking about? He's my best friend. He's done me the greatest service in the world." He held her away from him, his fingers gripping her strongly, and she was aware again of that blazing excitement. "What do you think? When I came round after banging my head I could remember. I know now what happened that night!"

She stared at him, feeling a rising excitement to match his surging through her.

"Are you sure? Quite sure?"

"Yes." He closed his eyes, the frown lines deepening between them. "I can see it all like a picture. Me driving round that blind corner under the thick canopy of trees meeting overhead. Do you know it?"

"Yes. Where accidents are always happening."

"That's right. Then I saw these blazing headlights coming straight at me on my side of the road. I tried to pull over, away from them, then I don't remember any more. I think it

288

must have hit me a glancing blow and sent me into a tree or something."

"You might have been killed," she breathed, appalled at the picture he had conjured up.

"I was lucky," he said grimly. "I must have been knocked out, then come round again later on and just driven home."

"Without realising what had happened?"

"Yes. Concussion does that sometimes."

She was silent for a while, shivering inwardly at the narrow escape he had had.

"So you weren't to blame, after all. All this need never have happened."

"No. All those wasted months," he said quietly, almost to himself, but she heard him and could hardly control the tears which constricted her throat.

"It's over now," she said gently. "What are you going to do?"

"Apply to be put back on the Register again, of course."

"And then?"

"Then I'm going to rebuild our marriage, my darling." His arms slid around her and he pulled her close to him. "We lost touch with each other over the last few years because I had to work too hard and left you alone too often. But now — you did mean it when you said you loved me? You did, didn't you?" he said again, urgently, fearfully.

She felt happiness begin to glow through her at his words.

"Yes," she said clearly, then as his arms tightened possessively round her, added quickly, "No, wait, darling. Listen to me first. Do you remember telling me you would never ask me again? That next time I would have to ask you? Well, I'm asking you, my dearest love. Humbly, and with all my heart."

"Shelagh," he said, and as his mouth came down on hers there was no need for him to tell her what his answer was.

WITH SOMEBODY ELSE
Theresa Charles

Rosamond sets off for Cornwall with Hugo to meet his family, blissfully unaware of the shocks in store for her.

A SUMMER FOR STRANGERS
Claire Hamilton

Because she had lost her job, her flat and she had no money, Tabitha agreed to pose as Adam's future wife although she believed the scheme to be deceitful and cruel.

VILLA OF SINGING WATER
Angela Petron

The disquieting incidents that occurred at the Vatican and the Colosseum did not trouble Jan at first, but then they became increasingly unpleasant and alarming.

DOCTOR NAPIER'S NURSE
Pauline Ash

When cousins Midge and Derry are entered as probationer nurses on the same day but at different hospitals they agree to exchange identities.

A GIRL LIKE JULIE
Louise Ellis

Caroline absolutely adored Hugh Barrington, but then Julie Crane came into their lives. Julie was the kind of girl who attracts men without even trying.

COUNTRY DOCTOR
Paula Lindsay

When Evan Richmond bought a practice in a remote country village he did not realise that a casual encounter would lead to the loss of his heart.

ENCORE
Helga Moray

Craig and Janet realise that their true happiness lies with each other, but it is only under traumatic circumstances that they can be reunited.

NICOLETTE
Ivy Preston

When Grant Alston came back into her life, Nicolette was faced with a dilemma. Should she follow the path of duty or the path of love?

THE GOLDEN PUMA
Margaret Way

Catherine's time was spent looking after her father's Queensland farm. But what life was there without David, who wasn't interested in her?

HOSPITAL BY THE LAKE
Anne Durham

Nurse Marguerite Ingleby was always ready to become personally involved with her patients, to the despair of Brian Field, the Senior Surgical Registrar, who loved her.

VALLEY OF CONFLICT
David Farrell

Isolated in a hostel in the French Alps, Ann Russell sees her fiancé being seduced by a young girl. Then comes the avalanche that imperils their lives.

NURSE'S CHOICE
Peggy Gaddis

A proposal of marriage from the incredibly handsome and wealthy Reagan was enough to upset any girl — and Brooke Martin was no exception.

A DANGEROUS MAN
Anne Goring

Photographer Polly Burton was on safari in Mombasa when she met enigmatic Leon Hammond. But unpredictability was the name of the game where Leon was concerned.

PRECIOUS INHERITANCE
Joan Moules

Karen's new life working for an authoress took her from Sussex to a foreign airstrip and a kidnapping; to a real life adventure as gripping as any in the books she typed.

VISION OF LOVE
Grace Richmond

When Kathy takes over the rundown country kennels she finds Alec Stinton, a local vet, very helpful. But their friendship arouses bitter jealousy and a tragedy seems inevitable.

CRUSADING NURSE
Jane Converse

It was handsome Dr. Corbett who opened Nurse Susan Leighton's eyes and who set her off on a lonely crusade against some powerful enemies and a shattering struggle against the man she loved.

WILD ENCHANTMENT
Christina Green

Rowan's agreeable new boss had a dream of creating a famous perfume using her precious Silverstar, but Rowan's plans were very different.

DESERT ROMANCE
Irene Ord

Sally agrees to take her sister Pam's place as La Chartreuse the dancer, but she finds out there is more to it than dyeing her hair red and looking like her sister.

HEART OF ICE
Marie Sidney

How was January to know that not only would the warmth of the Swiss people thaw out her frozen heart, but that she too would play her part in helping someone to live again?

LUCKY IN LOVE
Margaret Wood

Companion-secretary to wealthy gambler Laura Duxford, who lived in Monaco, seemed to Melanie a fabulous job. Especially as Melanie had already lost her heart to Laura's son, Julian.

NURSE TO PRINCESS JASMINE
Lilian Woodward

Nick's surgeon brother, Tom, performs an operation on an Arabian princess, and she invites Tom, Nick and his fiancé to Omander, where a web of deceit and intrigue closes about them.